This is the story of Jimmy Stoker and it's best that he tells it himself. It's an odd story that begins with an 'ending' and ends with a 'beginning'. But first things first . . .

THE GIANT GOLDFISH ROBBERY

A CORGI YEARLING BOOK : 0 440 86412 7

First publication in Great Britain

PRINTING HISTORY
Corgi Yearling edition published 1999

Set in 14/16pt Century Schoolbook by
Phoenix Typesetting, Ilkley, West Yorkshire

Corgi Yearling Books are published by Transworld Publishers,
61–63 Uxbridge Road, London W5 5SA,
a division of The Random House Group Ltd,
in Australia by Random House Australia (Pty) Ltd,
20 Alfred Street, Milsons Point, Sydney, NSW 2061, Australia,
in New Zealand by Random House New Zealand Ltd,
18 Poland Road, Glenfield, Auckland 10, New Zealand
and in South Africa by Random House (Pty) Ltd,
Endulini, 5a Jubilee Road, Parktown 2193, South Africa

Made and printed in Great Britain by
Cox & Wyman Ltd, Reading, Berkshire

The Giant Goldfish Robbery

Richard Kidd
Illustrated by Peter Bailey

CORGI YEARLING BOOKS

To Cathy

1

An Ending

Granny Stoker saw it first. She saw it in the tea leaves.

'There's to be an ending of sorts,' she announced one night during supper, 'and with that ending, there'll be a new beginning.'

Everyone stopped eating and looked around the table, biting their lips and trying hard not to laugh. Granny Stoker was renowned for her pronouncements.

'Go on, laugh,' she said, 'but the tea leaves never lie.'

'The tea leaves have spoken . . .' croaked Dad in a shaky voice, wiggling his fingers and squinting his eyes.

Granny gave him one of her hairy eyeball looks and I could tell Dad wished he'd kept his mouth shut, but he went on. 'No-one's suggesting they do, Gran, but isn't it all wishful thinking? I mean, it's not exactly spelt out in joined-up tea-leaf writing at the bottom of the cup, is it?'

'Should we clear away the dirty dishes then?' said Mam, trying to change the subject.

'Not just yet,' said Granny and she reached over and lifted Dad's cup to her side of the table. She held it in both hands. It must have been almost empty, because she swirled it round and round three or four times without spilling a drop, then she tipped it over into the saucer and drained out the tea that was left. She placed the cup down carefully, her eyes intent on the emerging patterns. For a while there was absolute silence. I slid off my chair, ready to sneak away and escape upstairs or outside.

'Well then, what do *you* see?' asked Granny, looking across at Dad.

I could tell that Dad was tempted to say something like, 'a load of old tea leaves', but he didn't. He crept round beside her, then Mam did, then I did, all waiting to hear what Dad was going to say, all with eyes fixed on the bottom of the cup.

'I *think* I can see a ship and maybe a little jug with a handle,' he said quietly.

'And there's a little tree with a wheel beside it,' said Mam.

'And a dagger!' I shouted excitedly. 'And a mountain!'

Granny just nodded.

'Well?' said Dad. 'What do they all mean?'

'You really want to know?' asked Granny.

'Yes! Yes!' we all shouted.

Granny waited for silence, then pointing with her finger she began, 'The *ship* means a letter from overseas and the *jug* means that you will lose something dear to you. The *tree* means that you will move to a new neighbourhood. The *wheel* means that you must hurry. The *dagger* means that some danger is threatening, but the *mountain* means that someone of wealth and power will help you in need. I think you can clear away all those dirty dishes now, Sally,' said Granny, smiling at Mam.

And nothing more was said about it, at least *I* didn't hear any more about it, but it seemed to make some difference because the following week Dad got the letter about the 'European Fishing Policy' and that's when it all began.

2

The Ship and the Jug

You see, Dad was a fisherman back then. It was a bit of a struggle. He had his own boat, the *Sally Ann*, named after my mam. It wasn't a big boat, not like some of them. It was quite small and painted blue and white. He'd be gone most of the week, but we'd always see him on Saturday mornings when the fish were landed at the quayside and there'd be an auction where they'd sell them to different fish shops.

Saturdays were great. Mam and me would get up really early and walk down to the harbour. The *Sally Ann* would be somewhere in amongst the broken jigsaw of bobbing decks and masts and cabins. We'd see who could spot them first – the boat and Dad in his black and red blood-splattered wellies and with silver fish scales stuck to his jeans.

When I close my eyes I can still hear the mad squawking of the seagulls, the slushing noises of the crushed ice and the whirring of the fork-lift trucks. I can see the rainbow shimmering of the herrings, the gold and black, glassy eyes of the freckled cod and the ghostly white underbellies of the giant skate. But it's all just remembered – imagined – in my head.

The letter about the European Fishing Policy was all about how too many people were fishing for too few fish. *As if we didn't know!* They offered to give Dad some money if he agreed to stop fishing. It was quite a lot of money, but in order to get it he had to break up the *Sally Ann* so that no-one else could use her for fishing. It made it really difficult. Like when they say, 'You've burned your bridges,' meaning you can't turn round and go back across. Only this was 'burning your boats' so that you, or anyone else, couldn't go back out to sea.

Mam and me thought it was daft. Dad called it 'radical' and Granny, for a change, kept quiet. I suppose she was thinking, 'That's the little jug you saw in the tea leaves,' meaning the one that meant you'd lose something dear to you. Maybe Dad was thinking the same. All I know is that

11

eight weeks later the *Sally Ann* was gone and we'd sold our house. Then with everything, including Granny Stoker, packed into two hired vans, we turned our backs to the sea and kept driving.

3

The Wheel and the Tree

Our new house seemed to be as far from the sea as you could possibly get. It was on the edge of a little village called Larkstoke. I remember the first morning I saw it. It was still really early. There was a lot of mist about, but instead of looking dreary and grey the orange sun made it look pale blue and exciting. The vans had struggled to the top of a hill and as they rolled down the other side the mist began to clear. It was like falling out of the clouds, and there it was – a village made of stone the colour of cinder toffee, surrounded by that much green it made you feel dizzy.

The air smelt sweet not salty, and I guess we all felt a bit like fish out of water. Dad threatened Granny that he was switching to tea bags.

He was only joking, but I knew that he was thinking we might have made a mistake. We all were.

Then Granny saw the tree – not in the tea leaves, but across the road from our new house. It was an old dead *Somethingorother* with ivy growing all over it. The thing was that the ivy made it look like a giant teapot with a spout and handle and everything. Granny took this as a sign and so did we. We'd done the right thing. After we'd unloaded the vans I went exploring.

Larkstoke village began at the bottom of a deep valley in the Wychford Downs and gradually worked its way up. Our house was halfway down the hill. There was a church at the bottom surrounded by massive dark green yew trees. It looked really ancient and in the graveyard some of the headstones were tilting over, as if they were jostling each other for space. They reminded me of the boats in the harbour and maybe because of this I followed the path through the graveyard until it came out on the far side of the church by a slow-moving stream that seemed to run through the centre of the village. It wasn't exactly the North Sea, but I'd found water.

4

Red Bellies

When you lie flat on the path with your face close to the water and keep very, *very* still, it's amazing what you can see. It's like a whole other world in miniature with loads of different things going on all the time. Best of all are the sticklebacks, especially the male sticklebacks with the bright red bellies.

If you watch long enough you start imagining the ripples are waves and the chickweed is giant kelp. Then the sticklebacks become huge red-bellied barracudas. With a net and a jam jar you can be out at sea all day long, scooping them up from the hidden depths, keeping them prisoner for a while and then letting them go.

After a while I made friends with one or two of the boys and girls who played around the stream. It was still the summer holidays and that was the summer I was hardly ever seen without a jam jar dangling from a piece of string. It was either sparkly clean or murky green and full of ferocious red-bellied barracudas. That was how I got my nickname, 'Jimmy Jamjar'. I didn't mind being called that, because I was the best at catching sticklebacks and the 'Jamjar' bit seemed to say so.

Sometimes, at the end of the day, when everyone else had gone home, I'd set a night line, like Dad and me used to do from the beach. I was just pretending really. It was only a stick and a piece of string, with a lump of bread stuck on a bent pin, tied on the end. There wasn't much hope of catching anything, but as Granny says when she buys her Lottery ticket on Fridays, 'You've got to be in it to win it!'

Most mornings I'd follow the path along the stream until I came to a long redbrick wall that hid the garden of the Old Manor House. There were six willow trees that had been chopped off at my height, all in a line, and by the first one the stream was a bit deeper than anywhere else. It was here that I set the night lines.

This particular morning I reached down to pick up the stick, which I'd carefully hidden in some reeds, when something caught my eyes. I followed the length of string curling through the water until it ended, not in a piece of soggy bread on a bent pin like usual, but in a flash of brilliant white. I couldn't believe it – I'd actually *caught* something!

Slowly I lifted the string from the water, not really believing my eyes, and there, stuck on the pin, was a perfect little fish with a head and a tail and fins and everything. Except it wasn't a real fish; it had been carved out of an apple!

Someone had gone to a lot of trouble. There was even a tiny piece of red skin left to make it look like a red-bellied stickleback. I took it off the pin and looked around. There was no-one about.

Then I put it in an empty jam jar, with some water to keep it fresh. By the end of the day I'd forgotten about it and almost lost it when I emptied out my day's catch of 'red-bellies'. It floated up to the surface and for a second I thought of just leaving it. But then I thought, 'No, I'll take it back and show Mam and Dad.'

5

The Dancing Gulls

We were settling in at home. Mam was artistic.
She'd painted the front room Mediterranean
blue; also she'd decided that Larkstoke needed
a craft shop, so she was working all day and
most of the night making clay models of things,
then rubber moulds, then casting the things in
plaster. When I came in through the front door
she was lifting a twelve-inch-high giraffe from
its wobbly mould. It was brilliant white.

On the mantelpiece there were fourteen
other giraffes in different stages of being
painted yellow with brown patches, and when I
looked around there were zebras and leopards
and elephants and lions, all propped up against
the walls, standing on newspaper while they

dried before being stacked in old cardboard boxes with tissue paper.

'It looks like London Zoo in here, Mam.'

'I've been busy,' she said. 'What about you?'

'Oh, just fishing,' I said. I was going to show her the apple but it didn't seem so important any more. 'Where's Dad?'

'In the greenhouse. Where else?' said Mam. 'He hasn't got his "land legs" yet. Go and have a chat with him. I think he misses the fishing.'

I walked out into the garden. You could see where Dad had been. Everything was weeded, dug over and laid out in neat rows – potatoes, onions, lettuce, carrots – all neatly labelled with names like *Pentland Javelin, Maris Piper* and *Little Gem*. At the bottom of the garden was the greenhouse. Dad was sitting on a stool, re-potting some tomato plants. He had the radio on and I could hear the familiar voice of the lady who reads the shipping forecast: *'There are warnings of storms in Forties, Forth, Tyne and Dogger . . .'*

'I wouldn't want to be out there tonight,' said Dad with a sigh, pushing his thumbs deep into the potting compost.

'Mam says you haven't got your land legs yet,' I said.

'Aye, well, I think she means I still hanker

19

after the sea. A life on the ocean wave and all that nonsense.'

And then he paused, listening to the radio . . . *'Precipitation within sight. One thousand and four, falling more slowly.'*

'She's not wrong – your mam, that is. It takes time to get all that salt water out of your blood. I suppose as long as the moon pulls the tides I'll still be feeling the pull of the sea. But – you've got to move on. How's the Serengeti Game Reserve getting on?' And he switched off the radio.

'I told her it looked like London Zoo,' I said.

Dad laughed. Somewhere in the field beyond the garden a cock pheasant rose noisily into the blue darkness.

'What a racket!' said Dad. 'It sounds like a rusty clockwork toy.'

It was quiet for a bit, then Dad said, 'You know what I miss? I miss seeing the fulmars and the stormy petrels skimming across the waves. I *even* miss the noise of the gulls, and I never thought I'd miss that.'

'And the gannets diving!' I said. 'And do you remember how the seagulls used to land on the roof on the shed and waddle about like they were dancing?'

'Yes, *The Dancing Gulls*. Now there's an idea for your mam! She could do them in plaster and give them red satin dresses and fishnet tights. Come on, let's go on inside and give her a hand mucking out the animals. But don't sit still too long or you'll end up being painted with spots or stripes or patches.'

'Dad,' I said, fingering the carved apple fish that had now begun to turn brown and fall to bits.

'Yes?'

'Oh . . . nothing.'

We walked back down the garden path towards the light in the kitchen. Upstairs I could hear Granny's gramophone. Fats Domino was singing 'Blueberry Hill'.

6

The Stickleback King

The summer holidays were almost over. It was Friday, only three more days left, and it was raining. Granny tiptoed downstairs, too excited to bother with breakfast.

'Where're you off to, Granny? It's raining cats and dogs outside.'

'I'm off to get my Lottery ticket. I get one every Friday morning and I'm not going to miss it this week. Not after my dream.'

She'd had a dream the night before with loads of animals in it. She reckoned this was a sure sign that good luck was just around the corner.

'You've got to be in it to win it!' I shouted.

'That's right,' she said, closing the door behind her. I watched her struggle for a bit with her umbrella then patter off through the gate and out into the street that was shiny with reflected clouds. I waited for a bit. Mam and Dad were still upstairs, so I grabbed my waterproof, a net and a jam jar and went out.

On the way I started thinking about Mam and Dad and the craft shop. Dad really wanted Mam to have it, but it was going to use up all of the money he'd got from breaking up the *Sally Ann*. He didn't seem to mind. He just wanted to make sure that he was working and earning something before spending the last of the savings. He was trying to get a job as a gardener. He was brilliant with plants. Even by the sea we'd had a garden. Granny used to joke that Dad was born with webbed feet and green fingers.

Still, even with green fingers, gardening jobs seemed thin on the ground. Too many gardeners and not enough gardens – sounds familiar. Dad was in a pickle.

When I reached the stream, not surprisingly I was on my own. The rain had eased off a bit but the drops were still big enough to break up the surface of the water so that you couldn't see the bottom. It was a real challenge. *'There are warnings of storms in Rockall, Malin, Hebrides and Larkstoke.' I dragged the net backwards and forwards along the edge of the giant kelp forests. These were the best fishing grounds, teeming with shoals of red-bellied barracudas, but the*

23

storm was getting worse. Waves the size of houses crashed over the top of my boat. I could hear the wind howling. I could hear the timbers creaking under the strain. Would the net break? Would the boat tip over?

A welly full of water brought me back down to earth and I headed for dry land. After all that effort I hadn't seen a single stickleback, let alone netted one. I squelched along the footpath towards the Old Manor House. The sky was a shiny bright blue with dark clouds tumbling across it.

I crouched down underneath the first willow tree, where I usually set the night lines and where a couple of weeks earlier I'd found the apple fish. I watched the raindrops falling off the branches and plopping into the stream, making endless circles. It was like being hypnotized. The harder I stared at the water, the less anything else seemed to matter.

Suddenly there was a flash of turquoise, as if someone had chucked a can of baked beans from one side of the river to the other. It landed on an overhanging branch – a kingfisher!

I'd only ever seen one in books or on the telly, but now I could see the metallic blue and gold feathers shimmering as it pointed its bright red beak ready to spear. Then suddenly it was gone.

'They build their nests with fish bones

inside a burrow on the river bank,' said a voice behind me.

I turned, a bit startled, to see an old man with a big, curly, white moustache and small, round, gold spectacles.

'Had one fly smack bang into the conservatory window once. Broke its neck. Tragic, really. Couldn't decide what to do with it. Thought I might have it stuffed. Then I had the rather good idea of making some salmon flies with its feathers. That way it's still catching fish, in a manner of speaking.'

'Suppose so,' I said.

'Major Gregory's the name. But friends call me "Major Koi", on account of the carp.'

'Jimmy Stoker,' I said. 'But friends call me "Jimmy Jamjar", on account of the sticklebacks.'

'Ah, *Gasterosteus Aculeatus* – the three-spined stickleback. I remember fishing this stream when I was your age. I was known as the Stickleback King in those days.'

But then it began to rain again.

'Oh well. Best be off. Mustn't get too damp or the old war wounds will start playing up. Toodle-oo.'

'Bye,' I said and then watched him walking slowly back along the path, stopping every now and then to poke at the grass with the end of his walking stick. I could feel myself getting cold so I picked up my things and got ready to go back home. When I looked back along the path the Stickleback King had vanished – just like the kingfisher.

I walked back in the opposite direction. It was Friday night and that meant fish and chips for supper and being able to stay up a bit later than usual. Dad was reading me *Moby Dick*. We'd got to the bit where mad Captain Ahab was about to harpoon the great white whale and all the boats were getting smashed up and sinking. I couldn't wait.

7

The Other Side of the Wall

'And every time Moby Dick came back up, there was Captain Ahab, tangled up in his own harpoon rope on the whale's back. And his arm kept on flopping over like he was calling for all the others to follow him, except he was dead. And all the boats were smashed and sinking. It was fantastic!'

'*I know, I know*. You're preaching to the converted, Jimmy. I read that book to your dad when he was your age,' said Granny.

My head was still whirring with the story from the night before and I just had to tell somebody and Granny was the first up. I got on with my cornflakes and thought about what Granny must have looked like when she was Mam's age and then what Dad looked like when he was my age, and that got me thinking about the old man by the stream and how he just suddenly vanished.

I decided to look a bit further along that path to see if there was a door in the wall or something. Granny went back upstairs. I was on my own. I found a black felt tip pen and across the front of the cornflake packet, I wrote, '*Gone Fishing. Thar She Blows! Jimmy.*' Then I got my things and left.

I was right. There was a door in the wall, but it was locked. It wasn't as if I really expected him to be on the other side, but there was something in me that had to find out. I didn't want to break in or anything, I just wanted to see what I was being kept out of, so I looked round for a way over.

A bit further down the bricks were older and crumblier. The wall was still twice as high as me but there were places to put your fingers and toes. The first step off the path was the hardest. Then I was on the north face of Everest . . . *One false move and I'd be a gonner. I couldn't turn back now. The top was almost in sight. I was running out of oxygen and my crampons were slipping. There was a distant rumbling. It must be an avalanche! If I could just reach that last hold . . . Got it!*

I heaved myself over onto the top of the wall

and lay flat on my belly so that I wouldn't fall off. I suppose I'd expected a spectacular view, but all I could see was a mad tangle of branches and leaves and apples. I was face to face with the biggest apple tree I'd ever seen. It must have been hundreds of years old.

I thought about shuffling along, but there were some massive stinging nettles below and the top of the wall looked loose. I lay there for a bit and considered climbing back down, then realized that I probably couldn't. I was going to have to jump it. It was about then that I noticed the silvery flicker of water.

A good-sized branch was brushing against the inside of the wall. With the care of a cat on a pitbull's kennel, I lowered myself onto it. The branch sank down under my weight and some apples fell, quietly, into the nettles. A centimetre at a time I crept along its length, feeling like a fish that was hooked and being pulled in. The closer to the centre of the tree I got, the easier it became, because the branches grew thicker.

I could see the flickering of the water much clearer now. It looked like a big pond. I began to move out onto the far side of the apple tree so that I could get a clearer view. The further I moved out, the shakier it got. I was almost scared to move for fear of snapping something off. But there it was – the most amazing pond I'd ever seen.

It was more of a little lake really, surrounded by a beautiful garden. The whole thing was unlike anything I'd ever seen before. Around the edge of the pond was a stretch of white sand or gravel that had been raked into patterns, like waves. Here and there were biggish boulders, some just bare and others with moss growing on them. They were like islands poking out of a sea and the pond in the distance became an ocean.

Out in the middle there was a proper island. It probably wasn't that big, but it could have been Australia. It was joined to the shore by a curved wooden bridge that was painted bright red.

It was then that I noticed the massive orange heads that slowly broke the surface, swallowed, then sank. Forget Moby Dick. Forget the great white whale. These were great orange whales – a whole pondful!

I was so gobsmacked that I didn't hear the scratching of the rake beneath the tree. I edged forward, pushing my luck, and heard the sickening creak as the branch behind me began to snap.

8

Caught Red-handed

It's a horrible feeling when you know that you're going to fall, but you haven't quite gone. There isn't time to save yourself and yet it seems to take for ever. But once you start to go, you really go! *Wallop!* I was too shocked to feel really hurt. I hadn't broken any bones, but I knew I'd bruised my bum and scratched my legs. Apples were still plopping down around me and I was just getting my breath back when . . .

'Gotcha! Yer thieving little bleeder!' This old skinhead with grey stubble on his chin and gaps in his yellow teeth grabbed me roughly by the arm and dragged me up.

'Let go!'

'Not likely.'

'Let go or I'll tell me dad.'

'Tell yer dad? And what's he going to say about yer nicking apples then? What you need's a good clip around the earhole.'

'*Geroff!*'

'What's all this hullabaloo? Unhand that boy, Hackett!'

It was the old man I'd met when I saw the kingfisher.

'I caught him red-handed stealing the apples, Major.'

'No I wasn't.'

'He needs to be taught a lesson, he does.'

'I'll be the judge of that, thank you, Hackett. I do believe this young gentleman and I know each other. Let me see . . . Stoker, Jimmy Stoker. Or is it Jimmy Jamjar?'

'Jamjar'll do,' I said, not knowing where to rub first – my arm where Hackett had grabbed me, my bum that I'd landed on, or my knees that were all scratched.

'Wounded in the line of duty, I'll be bound. What say we hobble on over to the Manor together and share a pot of tea? Steadies the nerves.' We left Hackett, who I guessed was the gardener, grumbling beneath the apple tree and set off across the lawn towards the Manor House that looked as big as a castle.

'Sorry about that, Jimmy. Hackett was completely out of order shouting at you like that. I don't mind telling you that he's as rough on the plants as he is on trespassers and if it wasn't for the keen interest he shows in my carp I'd have given him his marching orders long ago.'

'I wasn't pinching apples,' I said.

'Of course not,' said the Major.

'No, really I wasn't. I just wanted to look at the pond.'

'And you're more than welcome. As a fellow fisherman my gates are always open.'

'The one in the wall was locked.'

'A-haaa. Then you shall have a key.'

9

The Manor

I'd never been inside anywhere that old or that big before. You could have fitted two of our house inside the first room we came to. There was a fireplace at one end that was big enough to walk inside and stacked up against it was a great pile of sawn-up tree trunks for burning. The walls were a kind of shiny blue-grey colour, dotted with paintings of old-fashioned soldiers in red uniforms with silver buttons. They were the highest walls I'd ever seen and ended with a ceiling that was covered all over in squiggly bits of plaster. It looked like we were standing inside a gigantic wedding cake.

'I think we'll take tea in my study,' said the Major. 'This way.'

And we walked through the first enormous

room and along a corridor with paintings and books and vases of flowers and doors that opened on to other rooms full of different things. My eyeballs were doing overtime. No-one was ever going to believe that I'd been here – that I'd seen all this.

'Here we are,' said the Major and he pushed open a door and stood to one side.

'This is my study – reserved for very special guests who appreciate the exquisite beauty of *Cyprinus Carpirio.*'

'Er . . . yes,' I said, wondering what he was on about, but suspecting that it had something to do with the pond and the great orange whales.

And then I twigged – Carpio . . . koi carp . . . 'Major Koi'. The pond was full of koi carp and this was his den – his shrine to the carp.

'Pull up a pew while I fetch the tea. Indian or Chinese?'

'Just Typhoo or PG, if you've got it.'

I sank back into an easy chair and felt my eyes slowly circling the room. And as they circled, carp began to emerge from every nook and cranny. Shiny orange and white carp floated in the pale blue glaze of an enormous Chinese vase. Heavy, dark green jade carp leant against a stack of books on either side of the mantelpiece. Paintings of carp so amazingly simple that a few strokes of the artist's brush had left a shimmering, living fish trapped in a paper pond.

I looked around and I kept thinking, '*like a fish out of water*' – that's how I felt. I'd never imagined in a million years that climbing that wall was going to get me this far and I had to admit that I didn't feel totally comfortable. Part of me wanted to be back by the stream, but part of me was taking it all in – lapping it up.

Across from where I was sitting was a glass cabinet that I slowly realized was full of the tiniest, most intricate carvings of carp and carp fishermen. It pulled me like a magnet, off the chair and across the rug, until my nose was touching the glass. These really did belong to a different world.

'The Japanese carve them out of ivory. A real eye for detail. Bit of a hobby of mine actually,' said the Major, setting down the tea tray.

My eyes wandered from the magic of the glass cabinet down to the table top on which sat the tea tray, a small bowl of apples, an open penknife and a stickleback carved from a slice of apple.

'Ah, yes. Caught red-handed. Always did like a bit of a joke. Hope you didn't mind.'

'No, I liked it.'

'Thought you might. Sugar?'

'Two, please.'

Somehow, finding out that he'd been the phantom carver of apple fish made everything all right. I didn't feel quite so uncomfortable. It was like we'd known each other for ages. I told him everything about moving here and where we'd lived before. About Dad and the *Sally Ann* and about Mam and her plans to open a craft shop and about Granny and the tea leaves. He laughed at that bit.

Then he gave me a key to the door in the wall and made me promise to come and see him next Saturday afternoon. He hobbled out to the garden with me and we walked back across the lawn to try the key in the door and make sure it worked.

'Best to check, then double-check. A stitch in time, etcetera,' he said, pressing up and down on his toes, as though he was trying to see over the wall.

'It works,' I said.

'Capital! Capital! Rendezvous at 1400 hours next Saturday.'

'To feed the fish?' I asked.

'To feed the fish,' he echoed. 'If there's any problem tell your parents to give me a tinkle. Three seven one's the number. Toodle-oo!'

I glanced back across the lawn to where Hackett was butchering a tree with an evil-looking pruning saw. I thought to myself, 'I've definitely made a friend, but I've probably made an enemy as well.'

10

Jumping to Conclusions

Monday morning and I was standing outside the school gates looking in. It was my first day at Larkstoke Junior and it was that feeling of falling all over again. Knowing there's nothing you can do about it. Feeling yourself go through the motions of escaping, but all the time walking deeper into the trap until it's too late. It was just because it was all new. Not just a *bit* new, but a lot new.

All the others had lots of friends, knew the teachers, knew where to go. I'd made a few sort-of friends fishing for sticklebacks but I couldn't see them anywhere. Mam and Dad had both offered to come along with me to the gates but I had to do this on my own. It would have been worse to be seen with your mam or even your dad, and Mam would probably have wanted a kiss! I started thinking about my old school and my best friends and for the first time since moving I really, *really* missed them.

But it wasn't that bad. I got teased a bit about the way I said things – my accent. But mostly it was friendly and good natured. By the time Friday came round I pretty well knew the ropes. I'd been picked for the school football team and we'd won our first match 4–2. I was walking back home a bit later than usual, with my football gear in a sports bag slung over my shoulder, when I saw Billy Gates and Sam Warner.

Of all the new people at school, these two were my least favourite. They had a bit of a gang. To be in it you had to wear the right trainers, watch the right things on telly and support the right footie team. It was daft and I didn't seem to wear, watch or support any of them. But then I didn't even *speak* like everyone else. In their eyes I was an outsider – I didn't belong.

Billy Gates was the leader. He was bigger than anyone in our class, but he wasn't very fast on his feet so he wasn't much good at football. Sam Warner wasn't much good at anything. I don't know how or why, I just knew I was in for trouble when I saw them and they saw me.

I was at the stickleback stream. I was

walking along the path kicking at the fallen leaves. They were up ahead, just beyond where the door was in the Manor House wall. They were throwing bits of broken branches up at the apple trees, trying to knock off the apples. There was no way round. I had to walk past them. If I'd had my key I might have sneaked through the door into Major Gregory's garden. But I didn't and anyway that would really have given them something to shout about if they thought I knew the Major. They'd probably have thought I was going to tell on them for nicking apples, which I wouldn't have.

'What're y'doing here, *Jamjar*? This path's private,' said Billy Gates.

'Since when?' I asked.

'Since now. That's right, isn't it, Sam?'

Sam nodded stupidly, pushing his spectacles up onto the top of his nose.

'This is me way home,' I said.

'*Me* way home? *Me* way home? What's wrong with yuh? Can't y'talk proper? Is that how *Jamjars* talk? *Me, me, me,*' said Billy Gates, pushing his face into mine.

Sam Warner laughed nervously.

'Look – let me past!' I said.

'Just told yuh, Jamjar. This is a private path. Either you know the password or maybe you could cross our palms with silver. How's about

41

fifty pence each? That sounds reasonable to me. Sound reasonable to you, Sam?'

'Cheap!' said Sam, taking his hands out of his pockets.

'I haven't got any money and I wouldn't give you any even if I had,' I said.

'Well, hop it then, *Jamjar*, all the way back to *Jamjar Land*,' said Billy Gates, poking me in the chest with his fat finger.

I felt myself getting hot and red. Billy Gates knew he'd won. The wall was on one side, the stream was on the other and there were two of them and one of me.

'Move it, Jamjar. Now!' he shouted, with his face that close I could feel his spit on my cheeks.

I was shaking with anger, but it wasn't worth the hassle. I'd take the long way back through the village. I turned my back to them and started walking, hitching my sports bag higher onto my shoulder.

'*Bye bye, Jamjar. See you next week,*' jeered the other two.

I felt like crying, I was that mad. I was thinking, 'They've won. I let them win. What would Dad've done, or Captain Ahab, or *Granny* for that matter?' Then it happened – *smash*! A bottle broke into hundreds of pieces on a stone just behind my legs. That did it! I threw the sports bag off my shoulder and ran back along the path.

Billy Gates was just standing there with his mouth open. Sam Warner had started to run off. I grabbed two fistfuls of jumper and with all my strength I swung Billy Gates round and pinned him against the brick wall.

'What yuh doing? Geroff, will yuh!' he said, in a voice that surprised me because it sounded scared.

'Why did you throw it?' I shouted, pressing his head against the wall.

'Throw what? I never.'

'Liar!'

'I never!'

'You try that again and I'll smash you.'

'Let go. It wasn't me – honest it wasn't.'

I let go and for a while we just stood looking at each other. Then he lifted his hand to feel the back of his head. There were tears in his eyes and brick dust in his hair. I wanted to say something else, but I couldn't think what so I just walked back along the path and picked up my sports bag by the pile of broken glass.

When I got home Mam was in the kitchen cooking 'Spag Bog'.

'Good game? Did you win?'

'Yeah, 4–2,' I said, dropping my bag on the floor.

'Excuse me, mister, this is the kitchen. Dirty football kit goes in the laundry room.'

'Sorry,' I said, picking it up.

'Take your mucky old boots out and that bottle of orange I gave you this morning.'

I opened the bag. There were the boots. There was the muddy kit. No bottle!

'There's no bottle,' I heard myself tell Mam. 'It must've . . . fallen out.'

'You'd have heard it smash if it'd fallen out, Jimmy. You must have left it somewhere. Never mind. Go on up and see Granny. She wants a word.'

What a twit! I felt so stupid. It had been my bottle. It had fallen out of my sports bag. Billy Gates was innocent – well, almost innocent. I trudged up the stairs to Granny's room.

'You look beat,' said Dad, who was coming down from upstairs, 'Hard game?'

'Yeah.'

'Hot bath'll do the trick.'

'Yeah.'

'Granny's looking for you.'

'Yeah, I know.'

Dad raised his eyebrows and gave me a pained look. 'Well, suppose I'll go and talk to me tomatoes,' he said.

'Sorry, Dad, I—'

'Doesn't matter. Really it doesn't. We'll talk about it later.'

'Thanks.'

Granny's numbers had come up last Saturday. Not all of them, but four of them had. She'd won seventy-seven quid, though you'd have thought she'd won the jackpot. I think she was happy mostly because she'd had the dream about all the animals the night before. And winning something – *anything* – proved her point. And four numbers wasn't bad. Nobody else we knew had ever got more than three. Anyway, she wasn't one to hoard it all away. She'd spent most of her life having to be frugal and the minute she got a bit extra, she blew it.

'Been out on the town, Gran?' I asked, as she opened the door in her best purple dress.

'Well, I've been *into* town and I got you this.'

She handed me a heavy bag. It was a book. I pulled it out. *The World of Whales*. It weighed a tonne. On the front cover a giant Humpback was breaking the surface. '*All the facts you'll ever need to know. Over 500 illustrations. 250 in full colour*.'

'Gran, it's brilliant, just . . . brilliant!' I slowly opened it and on the first page she'd written, '*Thar she blows! Have a smashing time at your new school, love Granny XX*.'

11

The First Visit

Saturday morning and Granny came downstairs smiling.

'You look pleased with yourself, Gran.'

'Tulips.'

'What?'

'*Tulips*. I dreamt of tulips last night. And tulips are very lucky. They promise abundance.'

Mam and me just nodded. We were all starting to take Granny's dreams seriously.

I spent the rest of the morning helping Mam around the house and Dad in the garden. I'd done all my homework the night before so after lunch I was free to meet Major Gregory.

It said ten to two on the church clock so I was a bit early. I dawdled along the edge of the stream. In the pocket of my jeans I could feel the key to the door in the wall that he'd given me. I stopped, took it out and looked at it. Maybe it wouldn't fit. *Maybe it would fit but there'd be nobody on the other side. Maybe the Major had forgotten all about me coming.*

I was at the door now. I stood still and listened carefully. I couldn't hear anything on the other side. Slowly I put the key in the lock and turned it. The door opened with a click. I took the key out, put it back in my pocket and stepped inside, closing the door behind me.

'Excellent! Excellent! 1400 hours. On the button.'

The Major was standing to attention with his left hand behind his back and his right hand lifted up so that he could look at his watch, which wasn't a little thing strapped to his wrist, but a big, round, gold job on a chain that he'd opened up and was holding in the palm of his hand. Without using his other hand, which was still behind his back, he snapped it shut and tucked it snugly into the pocket of his dark green and black tartan waistcoat. On top of this he was wearing an old orangey-brown tweed jacket that was patched on the elbows with bits of leather. In the top pocket was a neatly folded white handkerchief and stuck in the left lapel was a little twig of something purple that might have been heather. His trousers were made of the same orangey-brown tweed as his jacket. They were very baggy and fastened just below the knee. The bottom part of his legs was covered up with long woollen socks and on his feet he was wearing a pair of what Granny would have called 'sensible' shoes.

'Yes,' I said, not knowing quite where to begin or what to say.

The last time we'd met I'd said just about everything. There probably wasn't anything else to tell him. But I needn't have worried. The Major took charge.

'Good show. This way.'

He marched across the lawn. The grass had just been cut. Somewhere in the distance I could hear a big lawnmower grumbling and I suddenly remembered Hackett, but then forgot him again when we arrived at a beach of coarse white sand. It wasn't the kind of beach you would have just walked onto. It was obviously more for looking at than playing on.

'If the weather's fine I like to rake the sand first thing in the morning. Good start to the day. Clears the head. Puts things in perspective.'

'It's like the sea. The lines, the curving patterns – like waves,' I said, mesmerized.

'And the boulders?'

'They're islands. The moss on the top of them

is the hills and the sides are huge cliffs falling into the sea.'

'Indeed they are,' said the Major, sounding really pleased. 'I'm so glad you can see that. My gardener, Mr Hackett, thinks I'm completely bonkers, but then he doesn't have the same eye for detail.'

'Me dad says that you can see the earth in a grain of sand.'

'*And heaven in a wild flower*,' continued the Major. 'William Blake, *Songs of Innocence*.'

'No, Matthew Stoker, songs in the bath!'

We both laughed.

'Now let's be giants and stride across this swirling sea,' said the Major, lifting a leg in the air.

'But we'll spoil the patterns if we make foot-prints.'

'We won't make footprints if we use the step-ping stones. They're the large flat islands in a line over there. Don't worry, they're completely uninhabited so there's absolutely no danger of squashing any natives.'

I followed him across, him in his 'sensible' shoes and me in my trainers. Now we were right at the water's edge, and as if they'd heard us coming koi carp of all sizes and colours – yellows, oranges, reds and blacks – began to appear near the surface. It was amazing. I'd joked that they were like great orange whales. Of course they *weren't*, but some of them must have been nearly a metre long.

'Ah, my old gentlemen. They've come to see my young friend. General Patton, let me introduce you to James Stoker,' and as the words left his mouth the most enormous koi carp, which that was brilliant white all over with a silvery, greenish pattern of diamonds on its back, lifted its head from the surface and looked me squarely in the face.

'Did you say General Patton?' I asked quietly.

'Yes. All my oldest koi have pet names. I name them after military men as a rule. Something of a tradition. General Patton there has been with me since just after the war. That's over fifty years, though I don't care to think of it too much. He's what the Japanese call a *Gin Matsuba* or silver metallic, pine cone koi. Although I think General Patton's easier, don't you?'

'Yes, he's beautiful. I think I might have called him Moby Dick.'

'Ah, yes indeed. Great book. A classic if ever there was one, but rather an unruly mammal. Bit of a loner, what? Now by contrast the koi are disciplined. I like to think of them meeting in secret beneath the lily pads. Having the odd confab. Discussing strategies. Making plans for the campaign of the day. Organizing the troops.'

'Fifty years old! That's older than me dad.'

'Quite so, and somewhat unusual for a European specimen. Although they do claim that in Japan there are koi that are over one hundred years old.'

'A hundred! D'you believe them?'

'I have no reason to doubt it. We've had our differences, but the Japanese are an honourable people and they have been breeding koi carp for the beauty of their markings, the grace of their movements and their simple companionship for centuries. General Patton himself, like most of the other really old gentlemen, originally came from Japan. Just after the war that was the only place one could get hold of koi carp of real quality and many would insist that it still is.'

'Do people go all the way to Japan to buy a fish?'

'Not just any fish, my boy. We're talking about championship koi carp with unique and near perfect markings. The kind of koi that a serious enthusiast would gladly swap a large house and a smart car for.'

'Crumbs! There must be nearly a hundred koi in there. That's – that's – *millions of pounds*!'

'Well, they're not all tip-top champions, but many of the larger koi, my old gentlemen – the generals are international gold medal winners and virtually priceless. But then, how would you put a price on a friendship that has endured half a century?'

'I guess you couldn't.'

'That's right,' said the Major, digging deep into his trouser pockets and pulling out a handful of small brown cubes that looked like squares of fudge. 'Although some people, notably Herr Krumm, would disagree.'

'Herr Krumm?' I asked.

'Oh, just someone who thinks everything has its price. Austrian – terribly rich – clocks, I think he said. Chap thought I'd sell my generals. Must have been slightly deranged.'

He picked one of the cubes up between the thumb and forefinger of his right hand, slowly bent his legs and, with obvious difficulty, knelt down beside the water's edge. General Patton's enormous head reappeared almost immediately and the sad, fat mouth opened and then closed around the cube of food.

'Like to have a go?' asked the Major, holding out his other hand and offering me some of the food. 'I'm afraid I'm not going to be able to do this much longer. The "bending down" bit, that is. Old war wounds, don't you know.'

I took a cube and held it like he had, near the surface of the water. This time a different koi came up, almost as big as General Patton and white but with a huge dollop of brilliant orange on top of its head and two huge blue eyes. I looked into the eyes and thought about what those eyes were looking at. *They were looking at me.* It took the food. It was the strangest, most wonderful feeling. The only fish I'd ever got close enough to touch before now were the dead ones in the market, but here was this metre-long koi carp gently nibbling the end of my finger and thumb.

'Well, bless my soul, you are honoured! That was General Eisenhower, Supreme Commander of the Allied Forces.'

12

Dad's Bombshell

I said goodbye to the Major at about five o'clock. My mind was a whirlpool of koi carp and stories and funny-sounding Japanese names like *Goshiki* or *Kuchibeni*. The names were the names of the different types of koi. They described their markings, like five-coloured, mirror koi or red-lipped koi. There were hundreds of them. The Major knew them all just like he knew the names of his generals. I could remember the names of the generals, but the Japanese names were more difficult.

When I closed the door in the wall behind me it was like stepping out of one world and into another, but for a while, walking along the path by the stream, I was still in *The Land of Koi*. My feet were moving one in front of the other and my eyes were looking at the path and the water and the trees, but not really seeing them – not thinking about them. I'd never been abroad before – only to Scotland, and that doesn't really count, but I felt like I'd spent all afternoon in a foreign country.

When I got back home Mam was sitting at the kitchen table with a cup of tea.

'Hi,' I said.

'So,' said Mam. 'You enjoyed your afternoon then?'

'Yes. I had General Eisenhower eating out of me hand.'

'I thought he was Major Somethingorother,' said Mam, looking puzzled.

'No – I mean, yes. He is – Major Gregory, but General Eisenhower's a fish. A koi carp. They're all generals. All the really big ones. They're fifty years old and did you know—'

'Hang on, hang on. Just hold your horses a minute, mister. There's only so much a person can take in and I've had enough surprises for one day.'

It was when I slowed down and looked that I saw Mam had been crying. Her eyes were all red and she was sniffing a bit like she'd got a cold.

'What's wrong?' I asked her quietly.

'Oh, nothing really. Just your dad's dropped a bit of a bombshell.'

'Where is he?'

'In his greenhouse. Go on. Go and have a word. He'll be wanting to know how you got on.'

I went out into the back garden. The light was beginning to fade.

'Mam said you'd be in the greenhouse.'

'The doghouse more like.'

'Why's that?'

'She hasn't told you?'

'No.'

'Well,' he said, sipping from a can of beer, 'there's not that much money in the bank. At least not enough for your mam's craft shop.'

'But what about the money you got for breaking up the *Sally Ann*?'

'I never got that money, because I never broke her up.'

'*You've kept her?*'

'Yes, I couldn't – I just couldn't do it. I kept thinking of those quiet nights, sitting in the wheelhouse, riding a big black swell, watching the shooting stars and listening to the plop and hiss of a passing porpoise. I thought maybe – *just maybe* – if things worked out with the gardening I could save a bit and do her up. Convert her into a holiday boat and then we could still use her ourselves, now and then.'

'Dad.'

'Yes?'

'I'm glad.'

'Thanks,' he said. 'You know, I think when the dust settles your mam might be glad too, but right now I feel about as clever as the bloke who invented the chocolate fireguard.'

'Does Granny know?' I asked.

'She claims she knew all along.'

'Well, if she knew all along and she still came with us then it's going to work out. Right?'

'Yes?'

'*Yesss!*' And I gave him five.

There was a tap, tap at the door. We both looked round to see Mam standing with a tray of tea and buscuits.

'Can I come in?'

'Yes, yes,' we both said. Mam put the tray down alongside the potting compost. She'd washed her face and looked a lot better.

'Granny says they'll be picking the winning numbers in exactly three minutes,' said Mam.

We all smiled and picked up our mugs.

'And . . .' said Dad.

'You've got to be in it to win it!' we all shouted, clinking them together.

'Here's to Gran,' said Dad.

'And dreams of tulips,' added Mam.

13

Next Saturday

'General Patton and General Eisenhower you already know, of course, but that one there, the *Kuchibeni kohaku* with the red lips and the red and white markings, is Montgomery. I'm afraid he and General Patton don't see eye to eye. Never did really. Complete clash of personalities.'

We were standing together in the middle of the curving wooden footbridge at its highest point. The armrests and railings were painted a brilliant, shiny red and the whole thing arched from the edge of the pond over to the little island.

Looking down you could see some of the biggest koi weaving in and out of the water lilies.

'Ah, and there's the Desert Fox – Rommel himself. He's the *Hi utsuri* or red and black koi. A brilliant adversary. And General Zhukov, the *Gin kabuto* or silver-helmet koi. Another tricky customer with a terribly sweet tooth. He adored American Coca-cola. Drank nothing else, strange chap. Then there's General Gale, the *Kimbo* or golden-metallic koi and head of the 6th Air Division – Pegasus Bridge, D-Day, etcetera. Ah, and old General de Gaulle, the *Goshiki shusui* or five-coloured mirror koi. And last but not least, over there by the pink water lilies, the *Aka matsuba* or red pine cone koi. That old rogue, Lightning Joe Collins, Commander of the 7th Army Corps. Utah Beach.'

It was more of a history lesson than a nature lesson. I know it sounds silly, but I felt as though I was really meeting these famous generals.

'Do you have a favourite?' I asked.

'I shouldn't, but yes, I do. You might have already guessed. It's General Patton. I actually met the man, don't you know.'

'Really! You met the *real* General Patton?'

'Yes, right at the end of the war in fact. Charming fellow, if a touch flamboyant. But then most of the Americans were.'

'Oh, please tell me about him. How you met and all that.'

'Well, yes, let me see. It was right at the end of the war. 1944 in fact. We'd been captured in the desert a year earlier and after some pretty unpleasant goings-on we found ourselves in a German prison camp near the Czech border.'

'Did you try to escape?'

'But of course! We dug a tunnel from the bunk house under the exercise yard and under the perimeter fence. It took months and months. The tricky thing was getting rid of the soil. We made special pockets for our trousers which we'd fill with the tunnel's soil. Then when the Germans let us out for exercise we'd walk around the yard, kicking up the dust and surreptitiously letting the soil trickle down the inside of our trouser legs onto the exercise yard.'

'What was it like in the tunnel?'

'Not a pleasant experience. The only light you had was from a small candle and if that went out it was pitch black. You couldn't turn round, only go forwards or backwards on your belly. The walls were shored up as best we could with bits and pieces of packing timber, but every now and then you'd get a cave-in. Nasty business. Hellishly hot and dirty and all you had to work with was a spoon and your bare hands.'

'Did you escape?'

'No. I was the commanding officer. I stayed. Six of my men got out. One made it home, three were recaptured and two were never seen again. Missing presumed dead.'

'Was it really, *really* awful in the prison camp?'

'There were worse prison camps, much worse, but it was pretty awful. Not exactly five-star accommodation, what? No, no. It was a job to keep up morale. Having the tunnel gave the chaps something to work towards, kept them occupied. When the Germans found it – the tunnel that is – things got much worse. There was a price to pay. The only sense of freedom then was in dreams.

'I used to dream of sailing off the north-west coast of Scotland somewhere on a summer's evening. Alone with the Hebrides and the Aurora Borealis. And the chap in the next bunk used to talk endlessly about fish and fishing and how he was going to breed carp when he got back home. I suppose that's what got me started really. I'm breeding carp and he's probably sailing around the Hebrides somewhere.

'Anyway, at the end of the war we were all in a pretty bad way. Rumours were flying around that a German defeat was imminent, but no-one knew exactly what that would mean for us. Then one day we heard the rumble of armoured cars and in drove the American 3rd Army. They were unstoppable. They'd already crossed half of Europe and were on their way across the border into Czechoslovakia.'

'You must have been pleased to see them.'

'Indeed we were. The Germans surrendered without a fight. We'd just got over the shock when in marched a big man with enough coloured ribbon sewn to his chest to stock a modest haberdasher's shop. On each hip he carried an ivory-handled revolver. A Smith and Wesson .357 Magnum and a Colt 45. Just like a cowboy in the Westerns. "Who's the commanding officer here?" He asked with a hand on each hip. "Major Gregory," I said, introducing myself. "Major Gregory," he said, raising his right arm and saluting me, "you and your men have had a tough time. Sergeant!" he shouted at the sergeant who was busy taking down our particulars. "When can these men go home?" "We should have transport available in two days, sir," said the sergeant, jumping to attention. "That's not good enough. These men are coming with me *now*!" And with that he spun round and walked out. And that was General Patton. Old Blood and Guts, they used to call him. Nicest chap you could imagine. He was as good as his word. We were all flown back home that very night as guests on the General's private plane. I'll never forget him. He was killed in a car crash in 1945. Tragic, really.'

'Blimey!' I said.

And as we looked down, the silver shape of General Patton himself nudged aside a water lily pad and lifted his head quizzically.

'Enough about the war for today,' said the Major. 'How's your grandmother? Well, I trust.'

'Yes. She won ten quid last week on the Lottery. She got three numbers. That was the tulip dream. The week before she got four numbers. That was the animal dream. But she says that she's not going to waste her money this week because last night she dreamt of owls.'

'*Owls?* Are they terribly bad luck?'

'Only for a day or two.'

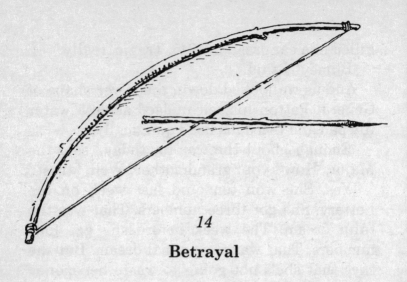

14

Betrayal

Over the next few weeks things seemed to fall into place, into a kind of pattern. Mam started working four days a week at the local flower shop, making up bouquets for people who weren't always sure what they wanted. Dad got a part-time job as a barman at the Two Birds, which he nicknamed the Dancing Gulls.

School was better too. Since the smashing of the bottle and me losing my temper with Billy Gates there hadn't been any more teasing about the way I talked. The word seemed to have got around.

I'd waited for him at the school gates on the Monday morning and when he saw me he looked really nervous. I went over and said I was sorry. I told him what had happened with the bottle in

64

my sports bag. He didn't say anything, just nodded and walked off.

In fact Billy Gates was much quieter with everyone. His gang started to dwindle, until there was only Sam Warner left. They never talked to me except if they had to and, whereas before I would have thought this was just great news, I began to wish I could be friends with them. It seemed daft to be in the same place all day long with someone and to spend all that time avoiding them. So the next Saturday, when I was walking along by the stream on my way to see the Major and I saw Billy and Sam, I didn't try to avoid them. I was early and had time to spare, so I walked up to them and started talking.

'Hiya!'

Sam looked at me and then at Billy. Billy was sitting on the path sharpening the tip of a straight stick with a penknife. Curly bits of white wood were falling on his trousers and beside him on the ground there was a bow made out of a strong branch and some string.

'I like your bow,' I said.

'We don't talk to *jamjars*,' said Sam, sniggering.

I looked down at my non-trendy trainers and thought maybe I'd better leave them to it. I kicked half-heartedly at a dead leaf and turned to go.

'Your dad was a fisherman, wasn't he?' said Billy.

'Me—? I mean, yes. He was. Why?'

'Did he ever catch sharks?'

'No, I don't think so. He'd sometimes catch dogfish which are like little sharks. But not on purpose. They'd just get caught in the net and usually he'd throw them back.'

'How's little's little?'

'About a metre or so.'

'That's *titchy*,' said Sam.

'Shurrup,' said Billy. 'Did he ever *see* any sharks though?'

'Yeah, loads,' I said, exaggerating a bit.

'Like Great Whites,' said Billy with wide eyes.

'I don't know about Great Whites but there was a Hammerhead landed at the fish quay once. It was a monster. Its eyes were on the end of great thick stalks where its nose was.'

'Do they eat people?' asked Billy excitedly.

'I don't think so. Me dad says they eat Stingrays but they're not affected by their stings.'

'I saw a bird eat a wasp once,' said Sam.

'Shurrup,' said Billy. 'Did you see that thing on the telly last night about killing sharks?'

'No,' I said.

'It was called "Blue Water, White Death" or

66

something. They lowered the divers over the sides in cages and threw dead horses' heads in the water and all these sharks went mad with the blood and tried to bite through the cages to eat the divers and the divers had to fire spear guns at the sharks to kill them.'

'I missed it,' I said.

'We're going to find some frogs to spear,' said Sam. 'Coming?'

'Frogs? With what?'

'With the bow and arrow, stupid,' sneered Sam. 'It's a spear gun really.'

'But *frogs*?' I heard myself say.

Billy just looked at the ground like he'd lost interest in the idea.

'Is it right that the old Major's your uncle?'

'No. He's just . . . just a friend.'

'And he's got a pond with giant goldfish in?'

'They're carp. Koi carp. They're like the biggest giant goldfish you've ever seen.'

'How big?' asked Billy.

I held out my arms at full stretch. 'This big . . . easy, some of them.'

'Wow! I wish I could see those. I'll bet they're pretty scary.'

'Not scary,' I said, 'just big.'

'Awesome,' said Sam.

'Just big,' corrected Billy.

And then I decided it. Just like that I said, 'I'll

show you.' And I knew, as soon as the words left my mouth, that it was wrong. That I should have asked the Major first. It was his pond, his fish, but I thought, 'It'll only take a couple of minutes and they'll have been and gone by the time anybody's there. And besides, it couldn't possibly do any harm.'

We walked over to the door in the wall and I took the key out of my pocket.

'You've got a key,' said Sam.

'What's it look like?' said Billy. 'Of course he's got a key.'

I opened the door and for a few seconds we all just stood still, listening and looking. There was nobody about.

'Come on,' I said. 'The giant goldfish are over here.'

I walked across the lawn with the other two right behind me until we came to the sandy beach with the stepping stones. The Major must have been out early, because the sand had been raked into fresh swirling patterns that were scattered here and there with yellow leaves, balanced on a crest or sunk in a trough like a fleet of small boats.

'Don't walk on the sand,' I said.

'Why not?' whispered Sam.

'Because it's – look, just don't. Use the stepping stones like I do.'

'Why?' asked Sam, nudging at the sand with the toe of his trainer.

'Follow Jamjar,' ordered Billy, prodding him in the chest with the arrow he was carrying.

We got to the end of the pond. It was strangely quiet. Normally the koi would have been swimming up to say 'hello', but there was only the waterlily pads and the odd 'plop' from further out.

'Look at that bridge! Cool or what?' said Sam.

'Where's the fish then?' asked Billy.

'Have you got any food?' I asked.

'Like what?'

'Like bread.'

'I've got a Mars bar,' offered Sam.

'Better than nothing,' I said. Sam unwrapped it and handed it to me.

'Just a few little bits of chocolate'll do.'

He took it back and broke off the end. I broke this up some more and threw it into the water, out from where we were standing. The chocolate just sank and we stood there watching the ripples it left on the surface.

'I thought everybody liked Mars bars,' said Billy.

'My Uncle Billy's got a budgie who eats Mars bars,' said Sam.

And then they came. Out of the murky green depths white, orange, red and black torpedo shapes nosed forward to investigate the sunken chocolate.

'Look at that!' shouted Billy.

'They're really big,' shouted Sam.

'They're awesome,' said Billy.

'They're not even the biggest,' I said. 'The biggest are twice as big and over fifty years old. These ones are probably just five or so.'

'Look at that white one with the orange spot on its head,' said Sam.

'That's a *Tancho*,' I said.

'It's a shark,' said Sam. 'A Great White and Orange killer.'

'Blue Water Orange Death!' shouted Billy, and he drew back the arrow on the string of his bow and pointed it down into the water.

'Watch out!' I said, but as I said it I heard the 'twang' of the string and the 'chomp' of the arrow as it pierced the water and bit into the side of the *Tancho* koi. There was a splashing and scattering of koi as they made their escape. All, that is, except the *Tancho*, which flapped helplessly on its side with the arrow swaying about in the air like the mast of a boat.

'No!' yelled Billy.

'You've killed it. You've speared it,' said Sam.

'No. It's still moving. It's not dead. I didn't mean to – I didn't—'

'Oi! You lot!' It was Hackett.

'Quick!' said Sam.

'Jimmy, I—' began Billy.

'Quick!' insisted Sam, tugging at Billy's arm.

Hackett was getting closer. Billy dropped the bow and ran off with Sam across the gravel, over the grass and through the door in the wall. I just sat there. I didn't even think of running away. I wasn't thinking about Hackett or the others. I was just thinking about the *Tancho* carp, which was lying quite still on its side, its blue eyes looking scared and its mouth opening and closing like it was trying to say something but couldn't. I knelt down and gently touched its head. It was going to die and it was my fault.

'You'll cop it this time!' sneered Hackett, staring down at the dying fish. 'That's the end of you, matey.'

But his words didn't really sink in. Like him I was watching the *Tancho* koi die, helpless to do anything.

'What's all the commotion?'

It was the Major. No-one said anything. I was kneeling down and Hackett was stood over me. The Major limped over and joined us and when he saw the *Tancho* koi and the arrow I could tell he didn't believe what he was looking at.

'It was him. This bloody kid. This mate of yours. He shot the koi with this bow and arrow.'

I looked up at Hackett. He was holding Billy's bow.

'It wasn't me,' I said feebly, feeling hot, salty tears beginning to run down my cheeks.

'So who was it then? Bloody Robin Hood?' sneered Hackett.

'I d-don't understand,' stammered the Major. 'How—?'

'I saw him do it!' shouted Hackett. And then I knew that Hackett had won, because in a way he was right. I'd let them in. I was responsible, even if Hackett was making out that I'd held the bow. I might as well have, because it would never have happened if I'd not been so keen to impress the others.

'I think', said the Major, as the *Tancho* carp gave its last gasp, 'I think you'd better leave. I don't understand all of this, but until I do . . . I think you'd better leave.'

'It was an accident,' I mumbled, sniffing back the snot that always seems to run when you start bubbling. 'Here's your key,' and I handed him the key to the door in the wall.

The Major's face was so sad. We both looked back down at the *Tancho*. Now there were two spots on the pure white body: the big bright orange one above the head and a smaller, uglier red one where the arrow pierced the flesh and the blood leaked out into the water in a pale pink plume.

'It's dead,' said Hackett.

The Major's face turned almost white, as if he'd been the one to lose all the blood.

'I need to sit down if you please, Hackett.'

'I'll be going then,' I said.

'Yes,' said the Major faintly without looking up. And I left feeling sad and sorry and stupid and angry, but mainly angry and it was with anger that I slammed the door shut behind me.

15

Every Cloud

The weeks passed by and it was nearly Christmas, but I didn't feel very Christmasy. The anger had gone away but the sadness was still there. I really missed the koi carp, especially the generals, and I really missed the Major and his stories. Every time the phone rang or the postman dropped a letter through the letter box I kept on hoping it was from the Major, saying that it'd all been a big mistake and that he'd be expecting me next Saturday. But it never happened. I thought about writing and trying to explain everything, but that never happened either. Every time I picked up the pen I'd get a lump in my throat just thinking about the dead koi.

At school Billy Gates took me by surprise. He

came straight over as soon as he saw me on the Monday morning after the shooting and asked me what had happened. Had I got away? When I told him I had just stayed there and then about the Major and Hackett and what Hackett had said about me being the one to fire the arrow he was really angry.

'But it wasn't you, it was me,' he said.

'I know,' I said. 'But Hackett's got it in for me.'

'Why?'

'I don't know why.'

'Look. I'm sorry, Jamjar. I really am. It's not fair. It was me. I did it, but I didn't mean to. It just slipped. I was mucking about and the arrow just slipped. It was an accident and you shouldn't have to take the blame. Why didn't you tell him it was me?'

'I don't know. At the time I thought, I let you and Sam in so it was me own fault, nobody else's. Besides, I knew it was an accident. I could tell that the arrow slipped and I didn't see why anybody else should get into trouble. If it had been just the Major then we could have explained things, but with Hackett there, sticking his oar in, we didn't stand a chance. Besides, I owed you one.'

'Owed me what?' asked Billy.

'The smashed bottle.'

'Oh . . . that,' said Billy. 'Listen, Jimmy, I'm sorry about giving you a hard time. You're all right.'

And so I found myself with a new friend. I wasn't part of the gang because I didn't want to be. Whatever else had happened I was still me. I kept quiet about the whole business for the rest of the term. I never mentioned it once until I got back home from school on the Friday afternoon that we broke up for Christmas.

'Major Gregory's been taken ill. He's in Wychford Hospital,' said Mam.

'How do you know?' I asked, getting my breath back after running.

'Well, a very nice lady came into the florist today and asked me to make up a bouquet of roses and daisies for Major Gregory and it was to be delivered to Wychford Hospital.'

'Maybe it's a different Major Gregory,' I suggested.

'No, I think it's your Major Gregory. The lady said that he'd probably have preferred water lilies.'

'That's him,' I said.

'But don't worry, it doesn't sound like anything serious. I think it was just his legs playing up. She said he was definitely hobbling home at the weekend, maybe even tomorrow, and she asked if we could make sure that the flowers got there today.'

I don't know why, or how, but I just knew everything would be back to normal when I next saw the Major. But I'd got no idea what I'd have to go through before then.

16

A Chance Encounter

'Winter's on its way,' said Dad as he came into the kitchen, half hidden behind an enormous bunch of coloured dahlias. 'I thought I'd clear out the greenhouse and bring these inside. There's going to be a proper frost tonight.'

'Yes,' said Mam. 'I heard on the radio that it was going to fall to minus four. Now don't you all think it's about time we began decorating this place for Christmas? I've brought back a bit of holly and mistletoe from the shop and the tree's outside waiting to be carried in. And while we're on the subject, has anyone given any thought to what they want for Christmas dinner? There's still plenty of turkeys in the shops but if you fancy anything more exotic you'd better look sharp.'

'How's about owl?' joked Dad.

'No thank you,' said Gran. 'Turkey will do just fine.'

'Has your mam told you the news then?' said Dad.

'About the Major?'

'Yes.'

'I thought that maybe we could drop some of these dahlias by the Manor with a card some time over the weekend.'

'That's a nice idea,' said Mam.

'Yes. Let's do it,' I said.

'And dahlias are the perfect choice,' said Gran, who was scratching around looking for a pen to fill in her Lottery numbers with.

'Is that right?' said Dad.

'They're the flowers of friendship.'

'Well, that's a stroke of luck. Talking of which, has that owl in the teapot tree jumped ship?' asked Dad, eyeing the Lottery ticket.

'No,' laughed Gran with the pen poised over the numbers. 'I've just got used to it. It still hoots, but not in my dreams.'

'Thank goodness for that,' said Mam.

'What's for tea?' asked Dad. 'I've got to be at the Dancing Gulls by six and I'm starving.'

'Friday night,' said Mam.

'That's right,' said Dad. 'Who fancies whale and chips? Jimmy, here's a tenner. You go and

79

get the whale and I'll cook the chips.'

'We're out of spuds,' said Mam.

'I'll get some from the farm shop,' I said. 'How many fish?'

'Four,' said Dad.

'Three and a battered sausage,' said Gran.

'Three and a battered sausage,' echoed Dad. 'Take your bike and put your lights on. It's dark outside.'

'And icy!' said Mam.

'There's a full moon,' said Gran.

'Watch out for werewolves!' howled Dad.

'Put your coat on!' shouted Mam, but I was already out of the house and pedalling downhill with my lights on . . . *My sports bag was slung over me shoulder and flapping in the wind. I was five miles up when the warning lights on the control panel started flashing red. There was a heat-searching missile right on me tail. It was gaining fast. I swerved to the left. Swerved to the right. It was still there. There was nothing else for it. I plunged the nose of the Super Jet Hawkfighter down and broke through the cloud at a thousand miles an hour. I was trying to loop the loop but the earth was coming up too fast. I wasn't going to make it. I'd have to eject. There was just time to . . .*

The first stop was the farm shop, where I got a load of spuds just before they closed. Then

I set off through the village to MacMoran's with my sports bag, now weighed down with lumpy spuds, bouncing against my back. MacMoran did the best fish, but my dad did the best chips. He cut them big and thick. 'Battleship chips' he called them and he cooked them in beef dripping until they were golden in the middle and brown round the edges.

I smelt it before I saw it. I put my brakes on and, sticking my arm out to signal, I turned left and came to a stop underneath the neon sign MACMORAN'S FISH AND CHIPS. I leant my bike alongside the wall and pushed open the door. Inside was warm and cosy. Behind the stainless steel counter the hot fat sizzled quietly and behind the glass window on top the first of the battered whales glowed crisp and golden.

Everything was squeaky clean and on the wall a blue neon circle zapped marauding flies. Below it, a red plastic Santa Claus said, 'Merry Christmas and a Happy New Year to all our Customers.' MacMoran appeared from the kitchen at the back carrying a huge plastic bucket of freshly cut chips.

'And what'll it be tonight?' he asked in a friendly voice.

'Three cod and one battered sausage, please.'

'No chips?'

'No chips.'

'The fish are ready but the battered sausage'll take a few minutes.'

I sat down on one of the red plastic chairs and looked up at the telly. It had been surrounded by silver tinsel, but it was off. Then I looked across at the fish tank on the table. There wasn't much going on there either – a few titchy bright blue things and a couple of bigger ones that could almost have been sticklebacks but weren't . . . Sticklebacks! I'd almost completely forgotten about sticklebacks. My mind was still that focused on *Tanchos* and *Kinbos* and . . . My eyes followed the stickleback 'lookalikes' from one end of the tank to the other. At the end nearest me there was a plastic diver wrestling with what was probably a plastic octopus, and at the other end there were some rocks and a dayglo green Spanish galleon. In the middle, lying on the gravel like sunken treasure, were two chips that someone had managed to squeeze under the top cover. I wondered if MacMoran had noticed them and I started imagining what it must be like to be a fish living in a fish tank in a chip shop. The door swung open and in came Billy Gates with a blast of cold air.

'Hey, Jamjar. What's up?'

'Nothing, just getting fish.'

'I've gone off fish,' laughed Billy. 'Have you got any battered sausages?'

'How many?' asked MacMoran.

'Two with chips.'

'Two with chips coming up.' And he emptied the bucket of chips into the hot fat so that the quiet sizzle turned into a noisy, spluttering roar.

'Me granny likes a battered sausage,' I said.

'Sounds like a sound lady,' said Billy.

'I'll tell her. She'll be chuffed.'

'Is that your bike outside?'

'Yes,' I said.

'I'm on mine as well. Listen I've got to go back the same way as you. Why don't we go back along the path by the stream and through the churchyard? It'll be a laugh in the dark,' said Billy.

'OK.'

So we waited until MacMoran had wrapped up the suppers in neat parcels of newspaper then we packed them away, mine in my sports bag and Billy's in his saddlebag, and we set off into the night. It seemed much colder now after being in the warm chippy. You could see your breath like clouds of smoke. It was properly dark, but with a clear sky and the full moon there was a strange bluish light, a bit like the light in the fish shop that zapped the flies, and there were big black shadows – moon shadows.

The streets were empty so we cycled quite

fast, side by side, as if we were racing. I could feel the heat from the fish coming through my bag and warming my back. When we got to the path by the stream it was too narrow so Billy went in front. I thought that he'd be racing along this bit, pedalling like mad, but instead he was going quite slowly. When he got to where the door was in the Manor House wall he stopped dead and I almost ran into the back of him.

'What was that?' he whispered.

'What was what?' I whispered back.

'That!' he said.

I stood dead still and listened with my eyes wide open and my mouth tight shut. There was a splashing sound and a grunting and then a kind of muffled bark.

'Did you hear it?' asked Billy with his eyes almost popping out of his head.

'Yes,' I said.

'Well?'

'Maybe it's a werewolf,' I joked.

'There's no such thing.'

'I know,' I said, looking up at the full moon and trying to sound convincing.

The splashing continued interrupted by the odd grunt and growl.

'It's coming from the Major's pond,' I whispered.

'Can werewolves swim?' asked Billy.

'It's not a werewolf.'

'Then what is it? It sounds *big* enough whatever it is.'

'Let's take a look,' I said.

'Have you still got your key?' whispered Billy.

'No, but we can climb the wall.'

'How?'

'Over here.' We wheeled the bikes over to where the bricks were missing in the wall and where I'd climbed up into the apple tree the day that Hackett first caught me.

'I can't get up there,' said Billy.

'Stand on your bike,' I said.

Then I leaned mine against the wall and climbed up onto the seat so that my hands could just about reach the top.

'Look where you're putting your feet,' I said. 'Hold on with your hands and climb up with your feet.'

I got to the top before Billy and gave him a hand up. I don't think he'd done much climbing because he was more worried about falling off than meeting any werewolves.

'Don't look down,' I whispered.

'I won't,' he whispered back.

We could hear the splashing noise coming from over by the pond. It was much clearer from up on the wall and the grunting now sounded more like a person than an animal.

'Keep down!' I whispered to Billy and we pressed ourselves flat against the wall so that we could smell the moss and cement. The voices were clearer now.

'*Pull bloody harder, can't yer?*'

'I can't see what I'm pulling.'

'Then use a bleedin' torch.'

'I left it in the van.'

'Fat lot of use that is.'

That voice! That snarl!

'It's not a werewolf then,' whispered Billy.

'No,' I whispered back. 'It's worse than that. It's Hackett!!'

17

The Robbery

'Let's get out of here,' whispered Billy.

'I want to find out what Hackett's up to,' I said.

Billy looked into the dark tangle of branches and sighed.

'Look, you go back down,' I said. 'Get on your bike. If I'm not back in ten minutes go and get the police, or go to the Two Birds and tell me dad.'

Billy looked down at the bikes.

'I feel dizzy,' he said.

'Here, hold me hand.'

'No.'

'I'll lower you off.'

'No, I'm staying.'

'You don't have to.'

'I know, but I ran off last time and I'm not going to this time. Not if you're not.'

'Thanks,' I said. And I really meant it.

'So what are we going to do now?' whispered Billy.

The moon had gone behind some clouds and it was suddenly much darker. In the distance I heard Hackett's voice again.

'I've got your end. Go and turn the headlights on in the lorry but keep them dipped. We don't want a light show.'

'See this apple tree?' I whispered. 'We'll climb through the branches to the other side. They'll never see us in the dark but we'll be able to see them.'

'All right,' said Billy, not sounding terribly convinced. 'You go first.'

I lowered myself onto the nearest big branch, feeling it sag under my weight, and carefully picked my way through the smaller branches towards the centre of the tree. Billy followed behind. I'd forgotten how much heavier he was and for a nasty moment the branch creaked so that I thought it might snap or Hackett and his mate might hear it, but Billy was still there and Hackett was too busy to notice.

When we got to the centre of the tree I told Billy to sit still while I edged out a bit further. By the pond I could just about make out the huge, black rectangle of a parked lorry. As I watched, the red tail lights came on and the whole pond was suddenly lit up in a blaze of headlights.

'Dipped!!' hissed Hackett.

'Sorry,' said a voice from the lorry, dipping the lights.

But in that split second I'd seen the whole pond and I knew what Hackett was up to. He had a net stretched from one end to the other and was slowly pulling it in to the sandy shore where the lorry was parked. Leaning against the lorry were some nets on the end of poles, like those used for landing big salmon, and scattered about on the ground was a pile of big plastic bags and a red metal cylinder that was probably full of oxygen. I slid back down to where Billy was sitting.

'He's going to steal the Major's prize kois – his generals.'

'Why?' asked Billy.

'They're worth a fortune, that's why. We've got to stop him.'

'How?' asked Billy.

I thought about this. The idea of confronting Hackett didn't appeal. He was a nasty piece of work in broad daylight with people like the Major around, but alone in the dark didn't bear thinking about.

'Let's go back and tell the police,' suggested Billy.

'All right, but we've got to get that lorry's number. By the time the police get here they'll probably have gone.'

'You can't see it in the dark. There's no light on it.'

'I know. I'll have to get closer,' I whispered, lowering myself to the ground as quietly as possible.

'Where you going?' whispered Billy.

'To get a closer look.'

'But if you know it's Hackett we can tell the police and they'll find him,' reasoned Billy.

'I don't think he plans to come back,' I said. 'If he sells those koi he'll be rich enough to live anywhere.'

'Then I'm coming too.'

I thought it would be easier by myself, but there wasn't time to argue.

'OK, but *quiet*.'

There was a dull thud and Billy dropped to the ground with all the stealth of a Christmas pudding.

'Ssh!' I hissed and looked up expecting Hackett to be staring back, but no, he was too busy huffing and puffing with the last bit of the net.

'Right. I'll go first. Wait till I give you the

signal, then you follow. Keep low and try not to stand on any dry twigs or anything.'

'OK,' whispered Billy.

Over by the pond Hackett had the generals where he wanted them.

'Should I start filling the plastic bags?' asked his mate.

'Yeah. We'll do them one at a time. Pass that net that's leaning against the lorry and remember we don't want no damaged goods. We don't get paid for damaged goods.'

I waited until they were both busy, Hackett with the net and his mate with the plastic bag. Then, keeping my head down and my back bent flat, I ran over to a big rhododendron bush that was about halfway across the lawn. The grass was twinkling white with frost and every time my feet went down there was a little scrunching sound, but not enough to worry about. I could see everything that was going on much better from there, but that meant that they could probably see me too, so I was careful. The back number plate on the lorry must have been covered in mud because I still couldn't make anything out. I checked that Hackett was busy fishing and then waved for Billy to follow. He ran across the grass with his head down and joined me behind the rhododendron bush.

'Can you see it?' he whispered.

'No. We're going to have to get closer.'

'What are they doing with the fish?'

'They're lifting them out of the pond one at a time and putting them in those plastic bags that are half full of water.'

'Like goldfish at the fair.'

'I suppose so. Except some of those "goldfish" weigh over ten kilos each.'

'Then what are they doing?' whispered Billy.

'They're filling the bags up with oxygen from that red cylinder then knotting the ends.'

'Why's that?'

'It must be because they're planning a long journey,' I whispered. 'So that the koi have plenty of oxygen to breathe.'

I was all hunched up, making myself as small as possible, and I could feel my legs starting to get pins and needles. I moved my feet and stood on a dry twig. SNAP!

'What was that?' said Hackett.

'What was what?' asked his mate.

'Are you deaf as well as stupid? There's somebody out there.'

'Out where?'

'Out *there*. I just heard a twig snap.'

'I didn't hear anything. Maybe it was a cat.'

'How many cats you know snap twigs?' grumbled Hackett. 'I'm going to take a look around. Here, hold this.'

'I can't. It's too heavy,' moaned his mate, who was struggling with the first of the bagged koi.

'Useless—! Here, give it to me. Go and open the back of the lorry.'

Hackett lifted the bag onto the back of the lorry then jumped up and dragged it inside.

'What's this tarpulin for?' he growled.

'Dunno. Came with the lorry.'

Hackett jumped back down and took several steps into the darkness in the direction of the rhododendron bush. Then he stopped. The lights were behind him and his dark silhouette was shrouded by clouds of frozen breath, making him look seriously menacing.

'Perhaps you're right.'

''Bout what?' asked his mate.

'The cat,' said Hackett, grudgingly.

I wanted to heave a huge sigh of relief and say a quick prayer for all fat cats everywhere and I'm sure that Billy did too, but we didn't dare in case he heard us.

For the next half hour or so Hackett and his mate transferred the generals, one by one, from the pond to the back of the lorry, each one individually bagged with pond water and extra oxygen. The clouds had blown away and the full moon was shining with a vengeance. We couldn't get any closer to the lorry while they were going in and out of it and we couldn't run back across the lawn because now they'd be sure to see us. It was freezing cold and we both felt miserable huddled together underneath the rhododendron bush. All we could do was watch and listen.

'How many's that?' asked Hackett.

'Fifteen.'

'Leave the littler ones. They're not worth that much. It's just the big 'uns he's after. Old Krumm'll pay handsome for these old boys. It'll be like winning the Lottery, only easier,' and he laughed a wicked laugh.

Krumm? That rang a bell.

'Give us a hand with this oxygen and then pick up the rest of the bags and things. I want nothing left behind. Understand? Nothing,' barked Hackett.

There was a loud clunk as the cylinder was loaded back onto the lorry.

'Now we're going to get that net out of the water.'

'That's going to take ages and the water's bloody freezing,' moaned his mate. 'Can't we just leave it and get out of here?'

'Shurrup and do as you're told. I told you we're not leaving nothing.'

They both walked round to the front of the lorry then down to the edge of the pond and out of sight.

'*Now!*' I whispered to Billy, whose teeth were chattering loud enough to draw attention.

'N-n-now w-w-what?' he chattered.

'I'm going over to the back of the lorry to get the number. Wait here.'

'N-n-not bloody likely!'

'All right, but we've got to be quick.'

I ran with my head down until I reached the shadow of the lorry. Billy was right behind me.

'You keep a lookout,' I said and I went over to the back of the lorry.

The doors were still open and inside I could just make out the plastic bags piled together towards the back like a giant waterbed. There was also a big dark shape which must have been the tarpaulin that Hackett was on about. I looked down at the number plate. It had been smeared with mud, probably deliberately, but I could just about make out the registration –
E . . . 4 . . . 4 . . .

'They're coming back. *The other way!*'

It was Billy. What were we going to do? There wasn't time to run back to the rhododendron. They were coming back round the other side of the lorry. They'd see us.

'Quick! In the lorry,' I said.

I jumped up, so did Billy. We raced to the back and dived under the tarpaulin. I was sure Hackett and his mate would have heard us, but they were too busy arguing about the net.

'You do this my way, Shorty, or not at all. Get it?' threatened Hackett. 'Now get your waders on and give us a hand. It'll only take ten minutes. Then it's an hour to do the other pickup. That leaves all night to get to Dover. The boats not sailing till ten o'clock in the morning, so there's stacks of time.'

There was a scuffling at the bottom of the lorry. Presumably this was Shorty retrieving his waders. Then a few grunts while he struggled to put them on. Then the clump, clump of his footsteps and a thud as he jumped out onto the sand. All this time Billy and me had kept as still as statues underneath the tarpaulin.

'What are we going to do now?' whispered Billy, who could see that we were getting deeper and deeper into trouble.

'I don't know. Let me think,' I said.

It was just beginning to sink in how serious things were. There was no way we could jump out of this lorry without Hackett and Shorty seeing us. If they were in the water we might be able to outrun them, but if they weren't, well . . . no. We'd have to stay put and wait for a real chance to escape, but what we had to do, what we *must* do, was get a message to someone to let them know we were in this lorry.

'Have you got a pen or a pencil?' I asked Billy.

96

'No, I've just got a torch and a penknife and a bit of change from the chippy.'

The chippy . . . I suddenly remembered the fish and the spuds in my sports bag. It had been on my back all this time and I hadn't even thought about it. I took it off and opened it up. At least we had some paper, but without anything to write with that wasn't much use.

We'd had it. I hadn't a clue what to do. I just sat there staring at the parcels of newspaper: RUSSIAN SPACE STATION IN TROUBLE; SEX CHANGE VICAR TELLS ALL; TURKEY PRICES PLUMMET; DOVER–CALAIS FERRIES . . . BOOK NOW AND BEAT THE CHRISTMAS RUSH.

Dover–Calais ferries!

Yesssssss!

Quickly but carefully, I tore the advert from the page.

'What're you doing now?' asked Billy.

I couldn't answer him. My brain was working overtime. I was thinking, If I could get this message out of the lorry, then someone might find it. Someone with an eye for detail. Maybe the police, but probably the Major. He's coming back home tomorrow. If the shock doesn't kill him then he might find the piece of paper, but *how* would he know it was important and *how* would he know it was from me?

'Give us that penknife.'

'Why?' asked Billy.

'Just give it us quick.'

I reached into the bag and lifted out a medium-sized potato.

'This is a funny time to start peeling spuds,' said Billy.

'I'm not peeling, I'm carving.' I whispered.

'What're you carving then?'

'A fish.'

'*A fish?*'

'I've got to concentrate, Billy. I'll explain later.'

It wasn't much of a fish, not up to the Major's standard, but I knew he'd get the message if he found it. I wrapped the potato fish in the Dover–Calais advert and crawled over to the open doors. I could hear Hackett and Shorty huffing and puffing, dragging the net over the sand. I threw the little parcel into the darkness under the lorry and crawled back underneath the tarpaulin. The next minute the net was slung in the back. The doors slammed shut. The engine started up. And the lorry lurched forward, then sideways, then off into the night.

18

Kidnapped

When the lorry got going Billy and I crawled out
from underneath the tarpaulin. It was almost
pitch black in the back and every time the lorry
went over a bump in the road everything,
including us, would bounce up and down.

'Where's the torch?' I whispered.

'What?'

'The torch,' I said louder.

The noise from the engine just about drowned
out our voices so that if you weren't going to
shout, which would have been a bit risky, you
had to speak right into the other person's
ear. Billy reached underneath the tarpaulin
and pulled out his torch. He switched it on and
shone the bright white beam at the stack of
clear plastic bags each with its koi general

cocooned inside. As the lorry bounced the water sloshed, but there was barely any movement from the koi, except for the occasional flutter of a fin or flick of a tail. You could just make out who was who and I noticed, with mixed feelings, that facing us, with a puzzled look on his face, was General Patton.

I tried to explain to Billy why I'd been carving the potato fish and why I'd slung it under the lorry just before we drove away. He listened patiently, wanting to believe that it was a good plan, that it all made sense, but I could tell he thought I was as daft as a brush.

'But what if the Major doesn't find it? What if he doesn't even come home?' moaned Billy.

'He'll find it.'

'What if the lorry drove over it and squashed it?'

'Billy.'

'What?'

'Shurrup.'

Billy was really fed up and I couldn't blame him, so was I, but we had to keep our wits about us if we were going to get out of this mess.

'They'll find our bikes,' I said. 'They'll think we've been kidnapped by whoever stole the koi carp.'

'But we haven't been kidnapped. We're just stowaways. Hackett doesn't even know we're here and we haven't a clue where he's going or what he's going to do when he finds us.'

'If he does he'll be pretty mad, that's for sure,' I said. 'But he knows that if he does anything to us the police'll throw the book at him. Nicking fish is one thing but—'

'We don't even know where they're going, where they're taking the fish . . . and us.'

'I think I've got an idea.'

'Where?' asked Billy.

'Hackett mentioned a man called Krumm. D'you remember?'

'No.'

'Well, he did. Krumm tried to buy some of these prize koi from the Major a while ago. He offered the Major a fortune but the Major wasn't interested. I think Hackett has done a deal with Krumm. Krumm's from Austria so I reckon that's where we're heading. Dover to Calais, Calais to somewhere in Austria.'

'Great!' said Billy. 'I just popped out to get some chips and I end up in Austria. My dad'll be going spare.'

'Mine too. Look, I'm sorry, but you didn't have to follow me. I said back there on the wall that you could wait on the other side.'

'I know, I know. I'm here because I want to be, OK? It's just a bit more of an adventure than I bargained for and I'm still cold.'

'Me too and me bum's black and blue from bouncing up and down.'

We both laughed and looked around for something soft to sit on. Underneath the tarpaulin Billy found a couple of blankets.

'I'm starving as well,' he said.

'They're a bit cold but we've still got battered fish.'

'I've gone off fish,' said Billy.

'Oh, that's right,' I said. 'There's me granny's battered sausage if you want. I'm sure she won't mind.'

'All right then.'

So we shared the sausage, because somehow the idea of eating battered cod while the generals looked on seemed all wrong.

'We'd better switch off that torch. It's the only light we've got and it's going to be a long night,' I said.

We sat quietly in the darkness with our legs underneath the tarpaulin. After a while my eyes began to adjust and I recognized the ghostly white shape of General Patton staring back at me. I wondered what he was making of all this. He didn't look too worried, but then he was probably safer than we were. He was precious cargo and we were just stowaways. I started dozing off and I guess that Billy did too. I must have been properly asleep because

I remember having this awful nightmare.

We were both in the back of the lorry, except that instead of being under the tarpaulin we were in plastic bags full of water like the koi. I was in with General Patton and Billy was in with General Eisenhower. We were having a meeting about how to capture Hackett and Shorty and Krumm, when they all burst in and captured us instead. They put us in a metal cage and lowered us over the side of a boat until we hit the bottom of the sea. Then they dropped dead horses' heads all around us so that the water was red with blood and out of the red came great orange sharks. They were biting the bars of the cage, trying to get in and eat us. General Patton took charge. He said that we had to dig a tunnel. He said that it was our only chance, so we began digging from the bottom of the cage down into a black hole in the sand until we reached daylight and fresh air just before the great orange sharks broke into the cage. We were all laughing and shaking hands when we realized that General Patton had been left behind.

Then I woke up with a jolt as the lorry came to a halt and the engine was switched off.

'Billy . . . Billy!' I whispered urgently, elbowing him awake.

'What? What?' he said.

'Under the tarpaulin. Don't move a muscle.'

He said nothing, just did it. There was a lot of door-slamming and muffled voices. Then the engine started up again, moved slowly forwards, then stopped. The back doors must have swung open because even underneath the tarpaulin I could tell there was a powerful electric light shining on us.

'OK. Drag that net out and get rid of all that junk,' said Hackett.

'What about the tarpaulin?' asked Shorty, and my heart skipped a beat.

'Leave it,' said Hackett. 'We might need it to cover the fish.'

Someone, presumably Shorty, jumped up into the lorry and began to move things around.

'I can smell fish,' he said.

'Of course you can smell fish, Einstein! It's hardly bloody surprising with a lorry-load of koi carp.'

'Suppose so,' muttered Shorty.

'You better check them,' said Hackett. 'No, on second thoughts, I'll check them myself. You wouldn't know what you were looking for. When I think of all those months I took care of them like they were relatives or something, and that silly old codger thought it was because I liked fish! I'd like to see his face tomorrow when he sees his precious pond and finds his precious generals have done a bunk. "Hackett," he'll be

104

saying, "they've stolen my old gentlemen," but Hackett won't give a monkey's because Hackett will be filling his pockets with big, fat bundles of crisp Austrian schillings, thanks to that other idiot Herr Krumm. What a laugh. *Merry blooming Christmas!'*

'What's going to happen if Customs look in the back of the lorry?' asked Shorty.

'Nothing,' said Hackett.

'But they'll see the fish. Then what?'

'They're not going to see any fish, *dimwit*! They're going to see a lorry full of clocks with its export papers all in order.'

'How's that?'

'Because one of us, that's me, has brains. Now, assuming that sponge inside your skull can handle it, get in that forklift and start loading those boxes. Leave the fish where they are. I want the boxes packed wall to wall, floor to roof inside that lorry. Twenty thousand wind-up alarm clocks, delivered here last week from the Krumm warehouse in Vienna, to be delivered back to the Krumm warehouse in Vienna by us tomorrow. What a laugh!'

Under the tarpaulin it didn't seem funny at all. I'd forgotten that we weren't just dealing with Hackett and his mate. We were also dealing with Herr Krumm, who was much cleverer. This robbery might have been

Hackett's idea but it was being executed according to Krumm's plan. Hackett just wasn't that bright, even if he liked to think he was. But there had to be a way to foil the plan. *There just had to be.*

19

The Longest Night

We were moving again. Through the night and on our way to Dover. This time Billy and I weren't just locked in, we were trapped in the very back of the lorry by a solid wall of cardboard boxes.

'D'you think we'll run out of air and die like those people what get bricked into tombs in horror films?' asked Billy nervously.

'No chance. There's stacks of air, honestly. Besides, they didn't take the oxygen off. It's over there behind the bags of koi. If it starts to get really stuffy we can always turn it on for a bit.'

Billy just nodded. We were both tired. It had already been a long night and really it had just begun.

'How long's it take to drive to Vienna?' asked Billy.

'Dunno. Two days? Three days?'

'Three days! So if we don't suffocate we'll definitely starve to death. We'll have to become cannibals. We'll have to draw straws to find out who's going to eat who.'

'Billy, no-one's going to starve. No-one's going to get eaten.'

'I suppose we've always got the fish.'

'No-one's eating the fish.'

'Good, 'cos I've gone right off fish.'

'I know. You told me. Now listen . . . We know the ferry's not due to sail from Dover until ten o'clock tomorrow morning. They usually want you there on the docks about an hour before, but it's my guess that Hackett won't want to be sitting around Dover docks in this lorry. The police'll probably be watching all the ports and hopefully – although Hackett won't know this – especially Dover. No, I think he'll leave it until a bit later. He'll cut it fine and plan to arrive about nine-thirty, which'll give him just enough time to drive straight on if his paperwork's in order, but not so fine he'll draw attention to himself.'

'D'you really think he's that clever?' asked Billy.

'No, but Krumm is. Hackett's just following orders.'

Billy nodded.

'So what have we got? We've got Hackett and his mate driving this lorry turning up at the Dover docks. We're in the back, but no-one knows that for sure, except us. We can't just start screaming and shouting in case Hackett hears, 'cos then he might just drive the lorry to some back alley somewhere and we'd be for it.'

'Won't the police be searching cars and lorries?' asked Billy.

'Yes, there's a good chance they will, but all they're going to see in the back of this one is wall-to-wall alarm clocks and I don't think shouting's going to do us much good.'

'Why's that?'

'Haven't you noticed how quiet it is since the boxes? They must be acting like a soundproof barrier.'

'That's funny,' said Billy.

'What's funny?'

'The alarm clocks making it so quiet. They're supposed to make a noise and wake you up. Right?'

It took a couple of seconds for the penny to drop.

'Billy! That's it! You're a genius!'

'I don't want to be a genius. I want to be home in bed.'

'But that's exactly what we're looking for.'

'A bed?'

'No! A way to attract the attention of the Dover police tomorrow morning at 9.30. Something that'll make Hackett jump out of his slimy skin without letting him know we're on board.'

'The clocks?' said Billy.

'Yes. The alarm clocks. We've got twenty thousand wind-up alarm clocks in these boxes and even if we only managed to set two hundred of them for nine-thirty tomorrow morning, it'll be like Big Ben on wheels.'

'But what about the soundproofing?' asked Billy.

'We'll have to get them as close to the back doors as we can.'

In the light of the torch we gazed up at the smooth wall of cardboard. It looked impossible.

'Have you still got that penknife?'

'Yes,' said Billy, reaching into his pocket.

'Right,' I said, taking it from him and opening it up. 'There's only one thing for it.'

'What's that?'

'We're going to tunnel our way out.'

And that was the beginning of the longest night.

Each of the boxes must have been about seventy-five centimetres square. In the top right-hand corner there was some writing that said WECKER 100 ZERBRECHLICH! I think the WECKER meant alarm clock because there was a picture of a clock face and the ZERBRECHLICH must have meant fragile or breakable because there was a little picture of a broken wine glass. Then there was an arrow with OBEN written underneath it and a label which was stuck on and said KRUMM, FRIEDRICHSTRASSE 53115, VIENNA, AUSTRIA.

The wall was made up of twenty-five boxes altogether, five going along the floor and five going up the sides of the lorry. There was a bit of a gap between the topmost boxes and the roof, but it was much too small to crawl through and I didn't fancy getting up there and starting an avalanche of alarm clocks.

I stabbed the penknife into the end of the middle box that was on the floor and began to cut out a piece that was about forty centimetres square. The blade was sharp and squeaked as it cut. Slowly, like it was bleeding, tiny polystyrene balls began to spill out and roll across the floor. There was just a trickle at first, but when the cut cardboard fell away they gushed out with a hissing sound all over the place, revealing a stack of much smaller cardboard boxes that were white and about fifteen centimetres square.

I eased out the top middle one of these and opened it up. Inside was a clear plastic bag and inside the clear plastic bag was a stainless steel wind-up alarm clock with a little hammer and two bells on top, just like the one that Granny had in her bedroom.

'Should we try it?' asked Billy.

'What's the time now?' I asked, ripping open the plastic.

'It's five past eleven.'

I wound up the clock so that it began to tick and moved the fluorescent hands around until it said five past eleven. Then I set the alarm for seven minutes past eleven and gave it a couple of turns. We waited in silence like runners at the start of a race.

Tick, tick, tick . . . *DDDRRRRRRRRR* – Quick as a flash I wedged my finger between the hammer and the bell – *innggg!*

'Loud enough?' I asked.

'You bet!' said Billy, crossing his eyes and shaking his head from side to side.

We took it in turns. I emptied all the alarm clocks out of the first big box and Billy sat down in a corner. After checking each one against his wrist watch to make sure it was telling the right time he started winding them all up and setting them to go off at half-past nine. When the first box was emptied Billy crawled inside with the penknife and torch and started cutting his way through the back of the first box and into the front of the second. This took twice as long, and when all the polystyrene packing spilled out he had to shovel it behind him so that he could get to the next lot of clocks.

You couldn't really turn round inside the box. The space was too small. So after you'd got, say, six clocks you had to crawl out backwards not on your knees, but on your tummy, like a worm or a snake, dragging the clocks with you. Then you'd crawl back in and get some more and it went on like this until the box was empty and it was time to swap over and start again.

20

The Long Night Continues

Nearly five hours later, in the early hours of Saturday morning, the tunnel was six boxes long. Billy was winding up clocks and I was working on the seventh box.

Hackett and Shorty must have been taking the back roads to Dover because there were lots of twists and turns and we hardly ever heard any other big lorries, which we probably would have if we'd been on the motorway. All we could hear was the muffled drone of the engine. There wasn't a sound from the cabin up front. Every now and then they'd pull over and stop somewhere for a bit, but even then we couldn't really hear anything. It was like trying to listen to someone when you've got cottonwool stuck in your ears. Even so, when they stopped, so did we. We weren't taking any chances. We just sat or lay where we were and didn't move a muscle, didn't even whisper until the engine started up again and we all moved off.

The batteries in Billy's torch were starting to run out. The beam had faded from a bright white to a sort of yellowy colour. Luckily the faces of the alarm clocks were all painted with green fluorescent paint that glowed in the dark so that whoever was doing the winding up could see what they were doing while the torch went down the tunnel.

The further in we tunnelled, the scarier it got. It wasn't cold any more. Inside the tunnel was pitch black and hot. The blade of Billy's penknife was getting blunter with every box, making the job harder and harder. I was sweating and trying not to think about all those hundreds of clocks stacked above me, pressing down on what were now the empty boxes of our tunnel. Every time the lorry went into a bend the whole stack of boxes seemed to shuffle over. If you were inside the tunnel you could hear the cardboard creaking as the load shifted position. I could just imagine the headline: BOYS PRESSED BY TIME.

Even Granny would have had her work cut out spotting that one in the bottom of a teacup!

Granny! My mam! My dad! They'd be worried

sick. I wished I was home instead of stuck in a daft tunnel in the back of a lorry with a load of fish in plastic bags on the way to Austria. Still, at least Billy was with me.

As I slithered out backwards with the last of the alarm clocks from box number seven I thought I'd never make it. Every bone in my body was aching and my knees and elbows were dead sore from crawling in and out. The light from the torch was fading fast. It was definitely on its last legs and so were we. In the wishy-washy yellow light the back of the lorry was a strange sight. In one corner the plastic bags with the koi sloshed gently, while in the other corner, a silvery, ticking mountain of nearly seven hundred alarm clocks reached halfway up the sides of the lorry. The rest of the space was filled with a winter landscape of white polystyrene balls, crushed white boxes and crumpled polythene. Somewhere in the middle of this sat Billy, winding up the six hundred and ninety-fourth clock.

'That's it,' I said.

'Are we through?' asked Billy tiredly.

'Not yet, but that's the last of the clocks from this box.'

'I can't wind any more, Jimmy. My fingertips are red raw. I'm so tired I can hardly see the numbers. I want to go to sleep. I'm starving and

I want something to eat. I want to be anywhere but here doing this.'

'There can't be many more boxes. We must be nearly there.' And as I said this the wishy-washy yellow light from the torch faded to nothing and we were left sitting in the dark staring at what was now a fluorescent green, ticking mountain. Our eyes must have been adjusting as the torch was fading because it wasn't like everything just suddenly disappeared. To be honest, there wasn't that much difference, but the tunnel was now in *total darkness*.

'I'm not going back in there,' said Billy. 'I know it's my turn but I can't. Not now it's all dark.'

I looked at the entrance to the tunnel. I didn't fancy it either but I just knew in my bones that we were nearly there.

'Don't bother winding any more,' I said. 'We've got more than enough but we've got to get through to the back doors. I'm going back in.'

'Careful,' said Billy.

'It's a bit late for that,' I said.

'Suppose so,' sighed Billy.

I left the torch behind and with the penknife clamped between my teeth like some pirate I slithered back into the tunnel, pulling myself forwards with my elbows. It was black. So black that when I closed my eyes there wasn't any difference.

Below me I could hear the drone of the engine and above me I could hear the ominous creaking of cardboard boxes under pressure. This wasn't the kind of place to hang about. I kept slithering as fast as I could until my head banged against the end of box number seven. I stabbed the knife in and began cutting. In the darkness I could hear the hiss of the tiny polystyrene balls falling out into the tunnel, but I couldn't see them. The knife was so blunt that I wasn't cutting any more, just hacking. I tore the cardboard away and pushed the packing behind me. Then I started to drag out the clocks – one . . . two . . . three . . . I stuffed them behind me then got some more – four . . . five . . . six . . . I stuffed these behind me and kicked my feet to make some room.

. . . *ninety-eight* . . . *ninety-nine* . . . *a hundred!*
I was finished.

'Are you all right in there?' asked Billy, from what sounded like a long way off.

'Yes, but I'm stuck. I've pushed all the clocks behind me and I can't get out.'

'Stay there. I'm coming in.'

I heard Billy muttering to himself as he slithered to the rescue and then I felt the jumble of clocks behind me slowly start to move. I felt in front of my face with my hand and found the end of the box.

'If there's another one behind this we've had it,' I thought.

'I'll just drag some of these out,' grunted Billy.

'OK,' I said, lifting the penknife and stabbing it down into the darkness. It made a different sound – a dull thud. And as I pulled it out a thin shaft of early morning light pierced the darkness of the tunnel.

'Billy! Billy!' I shouted.

'What?'

'We're through, we're through! I've struck daylight!'

'Let's see.'

'You can't. There isn't room. Shift the rest of the clocks then I'll crawl out and you can have a look. But don't make the hole any bigger. If Hackett stops the lorry and opens the back for any reason I don't want him to see what we've done.'

It was half-past five in the morning. Outside the dawn was breaking somewhere on the road to Dover and in the trees and hedges, if there were any, the first birds had probably started to sing. But back in the lorry there was still work to be done.

'There's no need to ask what's next,' said

119

Billy, looking apprehensively at the fluorescent green and silver mountain of alarm clocks.

'No,' I agreed.

'Let's get started then.'

'I'll go first.'

'No, I'll go first,' said Billy. And he piled a load of fully wound up alarm clocks into the tunnel then crawled in behind them, pushing them all in front until he reached the end. Then he slithered back out and I did the same, slowly filling up the tunnel with 'live' alarms. We didn't get them all back in because they were all jumbled up, but we must have got about half of them in and the other half just made a smaller mountain in the back of the lorry.

'If you put a plate of bacon and eggs in front of me now I don't know whether I'd eat it or fall asleep on it,' said Billy when we'd finished.

'Bacon and eggs!' I said dreamily.

'Sausage and beans!'

'Fried bread and tomato sauce!'

'Spaghetti hoops!'

'Chocolate croissants!'

'Toast and marmalade!'

'Cornflakes!'

'Kippers!'

'*Kippers?* For breakfast?'

'Kippers and cold porridge. Anything. I'm starving.'

And we both laughed and lay down on the discarded packing.

'How long to go?' I asked.

'Till what?'

'Till the alarms go off.'

'Two hours and fifty minutes,' said Billy. 'Pity, I could have really used a lie-in.'

And he turned over and fell fast asleep. I just lay there for a bit longer trying to make sense of everything, but I was too tired. We'd been that busy that there hadn't been time to worry about Hackett, or Vienna, or Krumm, and now that we'd stopped I started thinking. But the thoughts were all in broken pieces and nothing made sense.

In the half light that now filtered in over the top of the boxes I stared across at the silvery-white torpedo shape of General Patton in his plastic bag. He was on his side a bit and lay very still near the surface. I could see the big black circles of his open eyes staring back at me through the plastic. I remembered my dad saying that fish don't close their eyes like we do and I decided he was asleep with his eyes open, dreaming the kind of dreams that koi carp dream. I tried to imagine what it must be like never to close your eyes and I felt my eyelids getting heavier . . . and heavier . . . until there was nothing I could do to keep them open.

I had this dream.

Me and Billy were trapped, except it wasn't in the back of a lorry, it was inside a giant alarm clock. It was dark and oily and there was nowhere to sit or get comfortable because we were squashed between huge springs and cogs and wheels and things that kept clicking and ticking and turning round. My mam was in there too somewhere, but I couldn't see her. I could only hear her saying, 'Don't you go getting that dirty oil on your nice new trainers,' and Billy was laughing saying, 'They're not the right kind anyway.' Then she was shouting at my dad who was outside. She was shouting for him to keep the hands of the clock still because they were going round too fast and the faster they went round the more we were getting squashed inside the clock. I looked through a tiny window and I could see my dad hanging from the minute hand with his feet dangling in the air, and Major Gregory standing on the hour hand trying to hook my dad's feet with the curved handle of his walking stick. Then Billy shouted for me to come over and look through this other tiny window, and when I did I saw Hackett and Shorty turning this big silver handle so that the clock kept going faster and faster, and they were laughing really evil laughs because they knew they were winning. And the cogs and the wheels and things kept closing in on us, and the windows were getting smaller and smaller, but just before they disappeared altogether I saw a tree in the distance that was shaped like a teapot and standing on top of it was Granny, and she was shouting something but I couldn't hear properly because of all the noise that the cogs were making. Then the winding seemed to stop for a minute and through the tiny hole I heard Granny's voice, ever so faintly, 'Where's my battered sausage?' 'We ate it, Gran,' I shouted back. 'Me and Billy had to eat it.' Then even fainter she shouted, 'Remember the tea leaves, Jimmy . . . remember the tea leaves . . . the tea leaves . . . the tea leaves . . . the . . .'

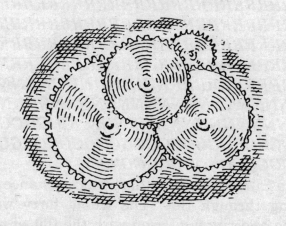

21

A Rude Awakening

*DDDDDDDDDDDDDDDDDDRRRRR
RRRRRRRRRRRRRRRRRRRRRRRRR
RRRRRRRRRRRRRRRRRRRRRRRRR
RRRRRRRRRRRRRRRRRRRRRRRRR
RRRRRRRRRRRRRRRRRRRRRRRRR
RRRRRRRRRRRRRRIIIIIIIIIIIINNNNN
NNNNNNNNNNNNNNNNNNNNNNNNN
NNNNNNNNNNNNNNNNNNGGGGGGG
GGGGGGGGGGGGGGGGGGGGGGGGG
GGGGGGGGGGGGGGGG!!!!!*

It was nine-thirty and there was no chance of sleeping through this. The whole lorry was rattling and ringing. Even with the flat of my hands pressed tight over my ears it sounded exactly like what it was – seven hundred alarm clocks all going off at once.

I could see Billy's mouth moving but I couldn't hear a word of what he was saying, *'What?'* I shouted, but I couldn't even hear what *I* was saying. Suddenly the lorry lurched forwards very fast and an avalanche of rattling, ringing alarms swept down and half-buried my legs. Billy and I were thrown back against the boxes and out of the corner of my eye I saw the poor koi, sloshing around as if they were in a storm force ten. Hackett hit the brakes and we crashed forwards into the pile of soft packing just as two full boxes of clocks tumbled off the top and crashed down where we'd been sitting.

The ringing began to fade away and we heard the gears of the lorry grind into reverse. It began to move backwards, but then there was a crunch and a tinkling and it stopped. Now we could hear other alarms going off, but they weren't ringing, they were *wailing*. They were sirens – police sirens! Followed by screeching brakes, squealing tyres and slamming doors.

'Billy!' I shouted. 'It's the police.'

Billy just looked up at the roof, closed his eyes and flopped back onto the polystyrene packing.

'This is the police. James Stoker, William Gates, are you inside?' We both heard the policeman's voice at the same time as a waft of fresh, cool air and bright sunlight squeezed

through the gap between the boxes and the roof of the lorry.

'Yes! Yes! We're in here.'

'Are either of you hurt or injured?'

'No.'

'Just stay where you are. Don't panic. We'll have you out very soon.'

'Don't worry. We're on our way.'

And with that me and Billy started to dig out armfuls of Krumm clocks from the tunnel.

'I hope they're shockproof,' said Billy.

'It's Krumm himself that'll need to be shock-proof now,' I said over my shoulder as we tunnelled our way to the front, tossing the clocks behind us.

The voices on the outside got clearer as we moved further down the tunnel. When we pulled out the last of the clocks it felt like swimming up to the surface for air.

'Here we go,' I shouted and I stabbed the penknife into the end of box number eight.

The cardboard burst open and I found myself squinting at a very surprised police sergeant and four constables who were waiting for the forklift truck to arrive to start unloading the boxes.

'Well I'll be – Quick! Over here. Give me a hand.' And they pulled us out like rabbits from a top hat.

At first my legs were all shaky and I could hardly see anything, because the daylight was that bright. But in my ears I could hear the mad squawking of the seagulls and in my nose I could smell that familiar salty tang of the sea. It was like coming home. Then through the squinting I started to see the flashing blue lights of the police cars, the scrunched-up parked car that Hackett had backed into, and beyond them the huge shape of the ferry with its gaping black hold into which the first of a long line of waiting lorries was starting to drive.

Billy was rubbing his eyes and the policeman was scratching his head.

'So how did you manage that?' he asked.

'We tunnelled through the boxes and set all the alarms off.'

'Ah ha! And whose idea was that?'

'His,' we both said, pointing at each other.

'How did you know we were inside the lorry?' I asked.

'Your parents reported you both missing last night. Wychford police searched the area and found your bikes outside the Manor. They searched the Manor but didn't find anything. Everyone was starting to fear the worst, as they say. There was even talk of dragging the pond. Then first thing this morning Major Gregory showed up. Seems he'd been in hospital for a spell. Anyway, at 0900 hours precisely, he rang up to report the theft of his prize koi carp and informed us that he had reason to believe that – James Stoker?'

'That's me,' I said.

'Inspector Telfor. Pleased to meet you,' he said, then continued – 'that James Stoker had been kidnapped by the koi carp thieves and that they were on their way to Dover in order to catch a ferry to Calais. I suppose he must have had some kind of ransom demand. He muttered something about a potato fish wrapped in newspaper. I do believe he took the whole business rather hard. Seems to have affected his memory. Getting on a bit, I suppose.'

'An eye for detail,' I said.

'Yes, indeed. An eye for detail. You have to have these days. Modern policework is all about detail. Dotting those i's, crossing those t's.'

'I'm bursting for a pee,' whispered Billy through clenched teeth.

'Can you wait until you get to the station?' asked the Inspector.

'No.'

'Constable, take Master Gates over to the terminal building and the gentlemen's conveniences. Master Stoker, what about you?'

'I can wait. By the way, the koi carp are in the

back of the lorry behind the clocks.'

'They'll not come to any harm now. Follow me. We'll wait in the car. Now, where were we? Ah, yes. As soon as we got the tip-off from the Major we put the port authority on a state of alert. We thought we might have missed you, that you'd caught an earlier ferry, but we decided to do some spot checks on likely-looking vehicles – lorries mostly. Yours was approaching the checkpoint in an orderly fashion, when every alarm that was ever made seemed to go off at once. The sides of the lorry were literally shaking. The driver and his mate panicked and we had them.'

All this time I'd never given Hackett a thought and now, suddenly, as we were approaching the waiting police car, there he was on the other side of the road. He was standing staring at me with his mouth hanging open like a dead fish. You could tell that he couldn't believe what he was looking at.

'Oh, don't worry about him. He'll not be bothering anyone for a long, long time. The courts take a dim view of kidnapping.'

'I wasn't,' I said.

'Good.'

Then Hackett seemed to lift his arm up as if he was calling for me to follow him but it was just another policeman clipping on handcuffs and pulling him down into the back of another car.

'I mean I wasn't kidnapped.'

'Wasn't kidnapped?'

'Me and Billy. We weren't kidnapped. We just sneaked onto the lorry when they weren't looking. We were trying to get the number. We were trying to stop them stealing the kois. It all got a bit out of hand. But honestly, they didn't even know we were there.'

'I see,' said the Inspector, who seemed bitterly disappointed that there hadn't been a real kidnapping. 'At least, I *think* I see. Perhaps you'd both better enlighten us further.'

When we arrived back at the police station the first thing we did was to phone home.

'Jimmy! Jimmy! *Thank God!* Are you all right?' It was my mam.

'Yes, honest. We're fine. Just a bit tired. I'm sorry I scared you.'

'Scared? I was at my wits' end, Jimmy. Really, you can't begin to imagine what was going through my head when the police found those bikes.'

'Sorry.'

'It's all very well being sorry. Honestly, if it wasn't for Gran I'd have blown a fuse.'

'Is Gran OK?'

'Gran? Gran's fine. Never been better. Your

130

dad and me were running around like headless chickens and she just made everyone cups of tea and kept saying, "Don't worry. Everything's going to turn out fine."'

'She was right,' I said.

'I can see that now, but at the time I could have screamed.'

'Is me dad there?'

'Your dad's on his way down to Dover with the Major.'

'Major Gregory!'

'How many Majors are there?'

'Me dad and the Major are coming down here together?'

'That's what I said. The Major picked him up just ten minutes after the Dover police first called us. They're in a big transit van. It'll take them four or five hours so they should be there just after lunch time. He's very nice.'

'Who?'

'Your Major. Obviously thinks the world of you. Though for the life of me, Jimmy Stoker, I can't think why.'

'Ma-m!'

'Only teasing! Everyone else seems to think you're a pair of heroes. I'm not so sure if scally-wags wouldn't be a better word.'

'But the Major – is he really pleased?'

'*Pleased?* I should say so. I think if he'd had a

red carpet long enough he'd have stretched it from Larkstoke to Dover. He kept on and on about your eye for detail and a potato fish or something. What was all that about?'

'It was – I'll tell you later. It's a long story.'

'I expect it is.'

'Mam?'

'Yes?'

'I love you.'

'And I love you too, Jimmy Stoker.'

'Give Gran a big kiss.'

'She's just popping out to get her Lottery ticket. Wait a minute, she's saying something . . . What's that? She says – are you listening? She says, *Where's her battered sausage?*'

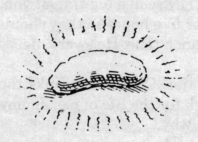

22

Right Off Fish

Luckily Billy's dad was more pleased that he was safe than mad at him for getting into trouble. Inspector Telfor brought us four doorstopper bacon sandwiches and two pint-sized mugs of tea. Then we were checked over by a doctor to make sure there was no 'damaged goods' and after that we sat down with Inspector Telfor again and went through the whole story from when we'd met at MacMoran's. I even told him about the chips in the fish tank, but he said that wasn't relevant to the prosecution. He was, however, very interested in everything I knew about Herr Krumm and the Major's prize koi.

He said that Hackett was making a full confession – singing like a canary, trying to save his neck. And that he'd already made a statement indicating that the theft had been masterminded by an Austrian industrialist called Krumm, who lived in Vienna.

'I couldn't for the life of me work out why a wealthy Austrian businessman would go to such extraordinary lengths for the sake of a few fish. But now that you've explained their immense value it's all beginning to make sense.'

'Are the koi safe?'

'Currently in police custody as, I believe, is Herr Krumm according to my colleagues in Vienna. Yes, he'll be finding that he has an awful lot of explaining to do.'

'D'you think he'll get away with it?' asked Billy.

'Not a chance,' replied Inspector Telfor. 'He might have got the likes of Mr Hackett to do his dirty work, but his hands are as dirty as anyone else's. We've got him hook, line and sinker, as they say. It only remains for Major Gregory to press charges and he'll be—'

'*Right off fish,*' finished Billy.

'Yes,' laughed Inspector Telfor. 'Right off fish. Very good, very good. Incidentally, there's one more task we'd like you to perform and that's to formally identify Mr Hackett and Mr Stonewall.'

'Mr Stonewall?'

'Otherwise known as "Shorty" Stonewall. Sometime long-distance lorry driver, sometime petty thief. Don't worry, you don't even have to be in the same room as them. We line them up with half a dozen other gentlemen of roughly the same age, height and build and you pick them out from the other side of a window. You can see them but they can't see you.'

'Let's go,' said Billy. 'Sounds like a good laugh.'

It wasn't much of a laugh. It was pathetic really. Hackett and Shorty looked so completely fed up and Hackett looked so mean with it that he might as well have stood in the line-up with a big 'guilty' sign hung around his neck. As it was there wasn't any difficulty in picking them out. It was just weird watching them through the glass window, knowing that they couldn't see you or hear you or touch you. It was like watching someone on telly.

In fact the last twelve hours or so had been that weird I felt like I was watching myself on telly most of the time. Billy said it was like when his dad took him to this Sealife Centre and they stood in the dark and watched these sharks swimming round and round in this huge, lit-up glass tank that went up and over their heads and down the other side so that they were in a kind of tunnel and the sharks swam right at them then over and down. Billy said that he felt sorry for the sharks because it must have been like standing outside a sweetshop when you've got no money.

I started thinking about how it was only a few weeks ago that the sight of Billy Gates coming towards me at school used to give me an empty, sick feeling in my tummy. I'd be expecting a push or a shove or at least a bit of teasing about the way I talked. I'd dreaded it. And here he was now, probably my best mate. I felt like I really knew him, like I understood him. Is that what happens? Is that why some people are always fighting? Because they're always like strangers without ever getting a chance to understand each other?

'I wonder if he likes cold porridge . . .' I said, nodding towards Hackett.

'I hope so for his sake,' said Billy.

'. . . and kippers.'

'D'you get kippers in the nick?'

'Dunno. But even if you did, I reckon he'd be—'

'*Right off fish*,' we spluttered, through the laughing.

23

Secrets and Promises

The police canteen was down some stairs in the basement. The first thing to hit you was the smell of food, then the noise – the laughing, the joking, the clattering of plates and the scraping of chairs.

When you stood at the top you looked down and out over a restless sea of blue uniforms huddled around different coloured tables that were all set at odd angles to each other. It reminded me of going down to the harbour on Saturday mornings with my mam and seeing who could spot my dad first. I got to thinking about the *Sally Ann* and how Dad still had her stashed away somewhere – not fishing, just waiting until he could do the work on her and convert her into some kind of holiday boat. And the more I thought about it the more I wanted to tell Billy about it, except Dad had made me promise not to mention it to anyone.

'DAD!'

It was my dad. He was weaving his way through the tables with Inspector Telfor, coming towards me and Billy. I jumped up and ran to him and he picked me up and gave me a hug.

'I'll see you later then,' said Inspector Telfor, smiling and then leaving.

'Dad, this is Billy. Me and Billy were in the lorry together. They've caught Hackett. We had a drive in a police car with the lights flashing and the sirens going dead loud. Where's Major Gregory? Didn't you come down with Major Gregory? Is he really pleased?'

'Hang on, hang on. *One* thing at a time. Nice to meet you, Billy.' And Dad and Billy shook hands.

'Dad.'

'Yes?'

'You know how I promised you I wouldn't tell anyone about the *Sally Ann*?'

'Ye-es?'

'Would you mind if I told Billy? I haven't told anyone else. Not since you said. Not even the Major.'

'I don't see any harm in that,' said Dad. 'Now, if you two have already eaten I'm going over to get meself some grub. I'll be back in two minutes.'

And he disappeared in a sea of blue uniforms moving roughly in the direction of the self-service salad bar.

'Billy?'

'Yeah?'

'Can you keep a secret?'

'Do ducks quack?'

'You know me dad was a fisherman before we moved to Larkstoke?'

'I know. You told me, or somebody told me. Why did you move anyway?'

'We moved because there just wasn't enough fish left in the sea. Not any more. Not since these great big factory ships started coming in from Russia and Spain and different places. There's nothing left.'

'But there's gotta be fish in the sea! The fish shop's full of them,' protested Billy.

'Yes, but the ones in the fish shop might have come from Norway or Iceland or Spain – anywhere! There's still some fish round here, but there's not enough for the smaller boats to make a proper living. You know the European Union thing?'

'Sort of. Why?'

'Well, they're trying to stop people like me dad from fishing.'

'That's daft. They should be stopping the bigger boats from fishing and leaving the smaller ones what catch less alone.'

'I know, I know. But they don't. They give people like me dad a load of money to smash up his boat so that he can't ever go fishing again.'

'This gets dafter by the minute! Is that the secret? That your dad had a boat, but smashed it up for the money?'

'No. The secret is . . . he *kept* the boat.'

'He kept the boat *and* kept the money?'

'No. He never took the money. He just stopped fishing but kept the boat.'

'What'd he do that for?'

'So that when he's got some money he can convert her into like a holiday boat.'

'*Her?*'

'Most boats are "hers". Ours is called *Sally Ann* after me mam. Billy, just think – we'll have a boat. A *real* boat that you can go all over in and sleep in and eat in and everything. And you can come with us sometimes. We'll go all over. We'll go up to Scotland and look for whales and sharks.'

'Can I? Can I really?'

'Yes! I promise. But you've not got to tell anyone about the boat. Not until she's fixed up.'

'I promise. Will we really see whales and sharks?'

'We'll definitely see whales. Me dad says there's loads in north-west Scotland if you know where to look. He wants to fit the boat up with underwater sonar stuff so that we can listen to the whales singing. Did you know that each male Humpback whale has its own song that lasts for up to thirty-five minutes and can be heard a hundred miles away?'

'You're having me on.'

'No I'm not.'

'And sharks?' asked Billy.

'There's Basking sharks.'

'Do they eat you?'

'No, but some of them are ten metres long and you can get in the water and swim alongside them.'

'No fear!'

'Honest. They only eat tiny shrimps and things, like most whales. There's Killer whales, but they just smash up icebergs so that the seals fall off into the water and then they eat the seals. I suppose it'd be a bit worrying if you were out in a small boat and a few of those started sniffing around.'

'I wonder what it's like getting swallowed by a whale,' said Billy, with a faraway look in his eyes.

'Probably not much different from being stuck in the back of a lorry with twenty thousand alarm clocks and a load of fish,' I said.

Just then my dad came back with a plate of salad that was that big it should've had a fence around it.

'Dad, where's Major Gregory? Mam said he was driving down with you.'

'He's just checking over the kois – his "generals", as he calls them. He's as pleased as punch with you two. Proud as can be. Says you're a pair of regular heroes.'

'Really?'

'Yes. Really. You'll be seeing him yourself shortly in Inspector Telfor's office. We're all meeting there at two o'clock.'

'Did he say anything else?' I asked.

'Can you keep a secret?' asked Dad, lowering his voice and widening his eyes that were peeping out from behind a huge forkful of lettuce leaves. 'Just until Christmas?'

'Yes,' I said.

'Because I want to be the one to tell your mam.'

'About what?'

'Well, we got talking, the Major and me. It was a long drive and mostly we talked about you and him and the koi carp. But we also talked about your mam and Granny and me and the fishing and moving to Larkstoke.'

'You didn't tell him about the *Sally Ann*, did you?'

'No, I didn't tell him about the *Sally Ann*, but we did get talking about gardening.'

'And? *Come on!*'

'Can't you guess?'

I thought I could, but I didn't dare believe it. It's like when you want something to happen that much you daren't say it. You've got to wait for someone else to say it.

'Go on – tell us.'

'Well, since the unexpected and sudden departure of his previous gardener, Sidney Hackett Esquire, Major Gregory finds himself with a job vacancy at the Manor. So . . .'

'You're going to be the new gardener.'

'You got it.'

'At the Manor!'

'The one and the same.'

'Fantastic!'

'Not bad, eh? I've told him I'll start next week, after Christmas. I'm going to keep on my bar job at the Dancing Gulls. So, in no time at all, we'll have your mam in her new craft shop.'

'And we can fix up the *Sally Ann* and go up to Scotland with Billy to look for whales.'

'Steady on! Let's not get carried away. First things first. Your mam's craft shop's the priority. It's no good getting all excited about whale-watching trips to Scotland until we've got a boat. And realistically, lads, that's still a long way off. Maybe years.'

'Years?' I said, unable to hide the disappointment in my voice.

'Perhaps,' said Dad. 'But mind,' he added, 'you never know what's round the corner.'

24

The Shortest Day

Inspector Telfor's office was grey. We sat on grey plastic chairs in front of a grey formica desk surrounded by grey metal filing cabinets. There was a small window out of which we might have been able to see the sky, but the grey blinds were closed and I decided that, even if they'd been open, the sky would probably have been grey on the other side.

The only bit of colour in the whole room was a framed photograph that sat on the Inspector's desk. It showed a lady dressed in a red coat standing in the snow and holding the hand of a little boy who was squinting his eyes tight shut. The little boy was wrapped up warm and had a bright yellow scarf round his neck and a purple woollen hat on his head. Behind them the sky was bright blue and I thought that they were probably the Inspector's wife and son.

In the dullness of the grey office the photograph stood out like a flower growing in a desert. I imagined him sitting there all by himself and looking into the photograph until the colours filled his head, so that in his imagination he was standing in the snow beside them until his feet got too cold. Then he'd jump back out again and be back in the office.

'Now that we have a parent present I would like you two boys to read through the statements you both made concerning the events of last night, and if they're all in order I'd like you to sign them just . . . there, on the dotted line.'

Billy and I both reached across for the pieces of paper and were reading through what we'd said when there was a bit of a commotion outside in the corridor.

'Who's the commanding officer here?' demanded a voice that I immediately recognized.

'Inspector Telfor, sir. That's his office just there.'

There was the sound of sensible shoes clumping on lino and then the sharp *tap, tap* of a walking stick handle against the door.

'Come in,' said the Inspector.

The door swung open.

It was the Stickleback King!'

'Major. Have a seat,' said the Inspector, motioning towards an empty grey plastic chair in the corner.

'If it's all the same I'll just stand at ease. Devil of a job getting back up again once I park the old posterior these days.'

And he took off his little gold spectacles and began to polish them with a red and white spotted handkerchief that he pulled out of the top pocket of his jacket. When he put them back on again we were all still looking at him. No-one had moved or said anything. It was like magic him being there in the same room. I held my breath.

'When can these men go home?' the Major asked the Inspector.

'There's just a few formalities to deal with and then we'll see what we can do about arranging some transport back north. I expect you'll be tired after your journey and could use a bit of a rest.'

The Major leaned his walking stick against the wall, spread his legs apart, opened his jacket and put his hands on his hips as though he was holding something that wasn't there. He glared back at Inspector Telfor, who was looking absolutely gobsmacked.

'That's not good enough. These men are coming with me NOW!' And with that the Major

spun round, picked up his walking stick and left the room.

'General Patton,' I said in quiet admiration.

'*Who?*' asked Billy.

'Old Blood and Guts.'

'You can say that again,' said the Inspector, looking blankly at the door, which suddenly opened again. This time just the Major's head appeared. He looked across and gave me a wink, then stepped back in, closing the door behind him.

'Profuse apologies, Inspector. A brief interlude of theatrical extravagance. Always thought I might have followed my Uncle Basil's footsteps and trodden the boards, don't you know. Bit too long in the tooth now. But not such a bad performance, what?'

'I – I – I'm sorry. I –' stammered the bewildered Inspector.

'Ah. But you wouldn't. No, indeed. The performance was mainly for the benefit of my young friend and confidant Master James "Jamjar" Stoker.'

'Star quality,' I said, smiling and shaking my head. And I was thinking *confidant* – I'm his confidant. That's great. That meant we shared secrets like me and Billy and my dad.

'Yes. Couldn't resist the opportunity to play the part of "The Great Liberator". It's rather a good story. I must tell you it some day, Inspector, but I expect you've got more important things to do than listen to an old man's war stories.'

'Unfortunately . . . yes,' said the Inspector, and I honestly think he meant the 'unfortunately' bit. You could tell that, like everybody else, he was really warming to the Major.

'Major Gregory,' said Billy, looking down at the floor.

'Yes, dear boy.'

'It was me what killed the carp – what shot it with the arrow. It wasn't Jimmy, it was me. It was an accident. I never meant to. It just – it just happened.'

'Water under the bridge, dear boy. Spilt milk and all that. If it wasn't for the vigilance and heroism *above and beyond the call of duty* that you two young gentlemen have shown I'd be the sorry owner of an empty pond. Indeed, I'm full of admiration for the pair of you. I have to say that the shooting of the young koi came as a bit of a shock, but I knew that something was up. You see, I noticed the footprints in the sand. They were most definitely made by two, perhaps even three, pairs of shoes. Completely different patterns. And when I came back to check on them an hour or two later Mr Hackett had raked the sand clear. It was then that I knew he wasn't telling the whole truth. You see, he *never* rakes the sand. He underestimated my eye for detail. I knew he was trying to hide something, but before I could find the proper opportunity to question him about it, my old war wounds started to play up quite badly, as they do once in a while, and I had to pop into hospital for a short spell. Of course, when I arrived back home I went straight down to the pond to pay my respects to the generals and saw that the sand had been disturbed by a very large vehicle. There were footprints everywhere, even in the frost across the lawn. I actually found your little parcel before I noticed the generals were missing so it didn't ring any alarm bells until I hobbled down to the edge of the pond and my generals were nowhere to be seen – and neither was Hackett for that matter. Then it all began to fall into place. I have to say that you made a remarkably good job of carving the potato fish, especially under what I imagine were rather adverse circumstances.'

'Thanks,' I said, feeling myself blush a bit.

'I expect you get your artistic talent from your mother,' said the Major.

'Well, me mam's artistic, but me dad makes great chips.'

'Then I expect it's from them both,' he laughed.

When everything was sorted we left Inspector Telfor's office and walked with him down to the police car park where Dad had parked the transit van that the Major had hired. Two police constables were carefully loading the last of the plastic bags filled with the koi generals into the back.

'Thank you for that, gentlemen,' said the Major.

'Not at all, sir,' replied the constables. 'Happy to oblige.'

'Are they all right?' I asked.

'Yes. Thanks to you and Billy. All, that is . . .' And his voice started to go a bit shaky. 'All, that is, except . . .'

'Not . . .' I started to say and as I said it my mind returned to the back of that lorry with all the clocks wound up and Billy asleep and me starting to fall asleep and I was looking across at . . .

'Not General Patton?'

''Fraid so. Every battle has its casualties. Let's just be grateful that it was, after all, a fish and not a person.'

'But General Patton wasn't just a *fish*,' I said.

'Quite. But this whole business has made me realize that people come first and that I must get my head out of that pond and look around me more often. Nevertheless he will be buried next

Saturday at 14.30 hours precisely with full military honours. I expect you all to attend. I'm planning a rather spectacular belated Christmas party afterwards. Give the old gentleman a bit of a send-off.' The Major paused and looked thoughtfully at the rear tyre of the transit van. 'Oddest thing,' he said, shaking his head.

'I expect it was the shock,' said Dad sympathetically.

'Very probably,' agreed the Major. 'It's just that Hackett's lorry had a collision with a car and the real General Patton died on December 21st 1946 after his car had a collision with a lorry.'

'*December 21st?*' said my dad. 'The shortest day of the year. That's today.'

25

A Beginning

We all piled into the transit van, me and Billy in the back seat and my dad and the Major in the front. My dad was driving. The Major wound down his window and we all shouted 'Bye!' to Inspector Telfor. He came over.

'Here. I almost forgot these. I shouldn't really – it's tampering with the evidence. So don't go telling anyone. I just thought you lads might like a little souvenir.' And he passed two small white cardboard boxes through the open window.

'It's not—' I said.

'It is,' said Billy. 'It's a *Krummy* alarm clock!'

'Safe journey!' shouted the Inspector, patting the side of the van with the palm of his hand.

I thought about him going back inside to his

153

grey office and I felt like shouting, 'It'll be Christmas soon. Everything'll be covered in snow. The sun'll be shining and the sky'll be a proper blue and you'll be able to go walking, just like in a photograph.' But instead I just shouted, 'Merry Christmas!' Christmas? It was nearly Christmas!

My mam would have the Christmas tree up by now and when we got back me and Dad would go up into the attic with a torch to look for the old cardboard box with the lights and the tinsel and the clip-on candles. Then when everybody was there we'd all decorate the tree starting with the lights, then all the shiny coloured balls and the funny little toys on strings, like red soldiers playing the drums and green crocodiles with Santa Claus hats on and yellow wooden camels and silver geese and reindeers. Some of them were really old and went right back to when Mam and Dad were little. It was one of the best bits of Christmas, unwrapping all the little toys for the tree after they'd been packed safely away, covered in tissue paper. It was like meeting old friends that you'd forgotten about all year and then suddenly, with Christmas, here they were again.

Every year we added one or two new ones, but somehow the old ones always seemed the best, as if they'd already been part of so many

Christmases that they'd soaked up more of the magic. There was even a fairy in a pink dress with gold wings that Gran remembered from when she was little, and I guess that the fairy had more magic than anything else because she always went on top of the tree even though she'd lost her wand a long time ago and the blue of her eyes and the red of her lips had all but worn away. It didn't matter.

'It seems like a dream,' said Billy, staring at his reflection in the face of his very own Krumm alarm clock.

'I know what you mean,' I said. 'I keep expecting to wake up in bed at home and there'll have been no lorry, no clocks, no tunnel, no fish.'

I loosened my seatbelt and looked over my shoulder. The blurred shapes of the koi carp – the orange, red, black and white torpedoes – all seemed to be facing forwards in their plastic bags filled with water, as if they knew they were going home. Or maybe they were staring at the big, blue coolbox, which I guessed wasn't full of cold drinks and fresh sandwiches, but instead carried a dead general on ice. Or maybe they were just asleep.

When I looked back round Billy was asleep. I carefully lifted the clock from his hands and put it down on the seat between us. Up in front Dad and the Major were talking about bonsai trees. Out of the window I could see the big blue motorway signs rushing towards us, then over us, then disappearing behind. The view on either side was flat and boring except for where the sun was setting over the Major's shoulder. The sky was icy pink and the sun sat on the horizon like a fat, red beach ball with a puncture, slowly going down.

Dad had turned on the radio and I could hear somebody talking about '*high ground*' and '*well below freezing*'. And then I started thinking about how I'd got my mam some dangly earrings for Christmas that were little silver fish on hooks and how me and Dad had secretly planted a hundred different tulip bulbs in the back garden outside Granny's window and that was going to be her Christmas present, except that she'd have to wait until the spring to see them. So in the meantime I'd got her a posh box of Chinese tea with really big leaves. But I still didn't know what to get my dad and I wondered if he'd like the alarm clock and then I wondered what I was going to get for Major Gregory and then I fell asleep.

I didn't dream, I just slept. When I woke up the van had stopped and there wasn't a sound. Nothing. It was definitely night time and the sky looked black, except there was a bluish light all around and a draught of freezing cold air was sneaking in from a crack where the door wasn't properly closed. The front seats were empty.

'Dad!' I whispered, looking around.

Billy was still asleep beside me. I undid my seatbelt and pushed the door further open.

'Sssssssssh!' said my dad, who was standing outside. 'Try not to wake Billy. But come and have a look at this.'

I clambered out of the van into my dad's arms. He lifted me up then put me down with a crackly *crunch* on the frozen snow.

'Wow!' was all I could say.

We were parked by the side of the road on the very top of the Wychford Downs. It had been snowing. The sky was alive with a mad twinkling of stars and behind us the almost full moon dazzled your eyes. The whole landscape was like a crumpled white blanket that was brightest and whitest on the hilltops, falling softly into blue shadow in the folds. Down in the very bottom, which was almost black, flickered the warm, yellow lights of Larkstoke village with tiny bright specks of red and green that must have been Christmas lights shining in the windows.

'It feels like a new beginning,' said Dad through a cloud of warm air.

'The first snow,' said the Major. 'I always think it makes it look as if everything's been temporarily removed. The decks cleared. Back to the old drawing board, so to speak.'

'Like rubbing everything out so that you can start again,' I said.

'In a nutshell!' agreed the Major. 'Starting again . . .' he sighed. 'Makes a chap think about all those things he resolved to do but somehow never got round to doing.'

'Like what?' I asked.

'Like exploring the north-west coast of Scotland in a boat, *alone with the Hebrides and the Aurora Borealis.*'

'Come on,' said Dad. 'Everybody down there will be waiting for the return of the conquering heroes.'

'Quite so. Quite so. After you, dear boy,' said the Major, holding the van door open while I clambered back inside.

Billy was still asleep. Dad started up the engine and we began driving slowly down the long hill, through the blue shadows, down to the warm yellow lights of home.

THE END

ALL TIED UP!
Mike Smit

'Run for it, Lisa!' I shouted. We ran, ran for our lives, charging through the streets of Whitby, the two men close at our heels.

Gangsters, bank robberies, kidnapping . . . That's not what you expect when you're on holiday in a quiet seaside town. But within twenty-four hours of unpacking, Robert and Lisa find themselves caught up in a wild adventure with a couple of bungling crooks on their tail.

One of the fastest and funniest holiday stories ever!

0 440 86372 4

CORGI YEARLING BOOKS

All Transworld titles are available by post from:

Book Service By Post, PO Box 29,
Douglas, Isle of Man, IM99 1BQ

Credit cards accepted.
Please telephone 01624 836000, fax 01624 837033
or Internet http://www.bookpost.co.uk or e-mail:
bookshop@enterprise.net for details

Free postage and packing in the UK.
Overseas customers: allow £1 per book (paperbacks) and
£3 per book (hardbacks).